BRAINWYRMS

Also by Alison Rumfitt

Tell Me I'm Worthless

BRAINWYRMS

ALISON RUMFITT

NIGHTFIRE

TOR PUBLISHING GROUP
NEW YORK

BRAINWYRMS

Copyright © 2023 by Alison Rumfitt

A Nightfire Book
Published by Tom Doherty Associates / Tor Publishing Group
120 Broadway
New York, NY 10271

www.tornightfire.com

Nightfire™ is a trademark of Macmillan Publishing Group, LLC.

The Library of Congress Cataloging-in-Publication Data
is available upon request.

ISBN 978-1-250-86625-7 (trade paperback)
ISBN 978-1-250-86626-4 (ebook)

Our books may be purchased in bulk for promotional, educational, or business use. Please contact your local bookseller or the Macmillan Corporate and Premium Sales Department at 1-800-221-7945, extension 5442, or by email at MacmillanSpecialMarkets@macmillan.com.

First published in Great Britain by Cipher Press

First U.S. Edition: 2023

Printed in the United States of America

0 9 8 7 6 5 4 3 2 1

Brainwyrms is a novel about the situation in which we find ourselves in the UK. When my first novel, *Tell Me I'm Worthless,* came out, some people noted that I included a content warning at the beginning. This is a content warning too.

Brainwyrms features (very) taboo sex that many would consider unsafe or unsanitary, as well as sexual violence and child abuse.

INTRODUCTION

My name is Alison Rumfitt and I am a cisgender woman. That's what I've decided. You can make that decision for yourself; it is perfectly possible. I've always been cisgender. I was born this way and I'll die this way. I don't write books about transness, nothing of the sort. My books, such as they are, aren't even about queerness (whatever that might mean). I don't write books about myself or things I've experienced. Any resemblance between characters in things I've written and real people is **purely coincidental***. I write horror and I write satire. I write purely for the entertainment of myself and others. Let me state it clearly: I am not subversive. I am a cisgender woman. I say this last part over and over to myself. I repeat it many times each day. My girlfriend wrote it down for me and she now helps me practise this affirmation, this plea. No ... let's start again. Let's not mention that I have a girlfriend. They aren't rounding up the dykes yet but with the way things are going I give it, what, ten years before they are. The other day in a café I heard a cis woman say to another cis woman in a hushed and serious tone, "Doesn't it scare you, Claire, doesn't it just feel like* The Handmaid's Tale *is coming true."*

I'm writing this right now in 2030, and if you're reading it then that's a bad sign. You shouldn't be reading this. It might mean I'm dead I suppose ... If I am, burn my shit. My partner might still be alive, and I don't want her to face persecution should these words fall into the wrong hands. If you, dear reader, are the wrong hands, then go fuck yourself. I hope you die. Kill yourself, etc. I'm sure that worked, so if you're still reading this it means you're not the wrong hands. Keep reading if you want to.

This country is a grey country. It has been grey as long as I've lived. Even on the hottest summer days it is grey, and in recent years two things have become certain: it's getting hotter and it's getting greyer. I'm writing this on 5 September, which, if you are reading this, I want you to note as an historic date. The UK government just put out a decree banning transgenderism. This doesn't personally affect me because, as I said, I'm a cisgender woman, but it affects a lot of people. It's scary. I'm scared. It's not really clear how they plan on enforcing this ban: perhaps, as some people on Newsnight *claim, the ban is only theoretical. How a ban can be theoretical they never seem to say. Perhaps the ban is only there to discourage and not to literally ban, which is something I'd believe more if it wasn't a literal ban.*

I've just been thinking a lot. About this mess and how we got here. I came out when I was twelve but even then, the Tavistock was basically a fucking traffic jam, each and every kid stuck but not suspended. With every passing day their bodies changed in the wrong direction ... okay, it was less like a traffic jam and more like a group of people stuck standing on an escalator moving down when they're trying to move up. I'm not really a cis woman, but let's keep that our little secret, dear reader. I got so used to coming out that I know I'll miss it, so let me do it one last time: I am transgender and I am a lesbian and I'm scared. I came out at twelve and finally transitioned at fifteen. I screamed at my Mother, saying that irreparable damage had already been done. What was the point. I'd always look like a fucking boy. And my Mum held me close and said that just wasn't true, the world was getting better. They were making progress every day. Even the Conservative Party just pledged to try and reform the process to make it easier for trans kids! That was then, and this is now: that future my Mother promised me never came to pass. I got my tits and my cunt, thank God. The Tavistock was bombed by a terrorist. The rest of the GICs were defunded little by little, year after year, until they barely had the money to treat the patients they already had, let alone take on more. Society in the UK – and worldwide, too – became obsessed with the spectre of the trans-sexual: the aberrant, abject societal glitch, the perversion, the rapid-onset virus praying on poor, defenceless kids. I knew that people didn't like trans people, but when I was a child that was sort of a background static buzz. During my transition, that background static buzz grew into an all-consuming scream. Loud enough to make your ears bleed. It spread from person to person like wildfire. It started with a couple of Guardian journalists and a sitcom writer, but soon their brain-eating transphobic parasitic mindvirus had washed across half of Britain's media landscape. Children's authors, news anchors, entire papers and magazines, musicians and directors. People who thought of themselves as well-meaning liberals were utterly consumed. Soon, they could only think of things in relation to trans people. Everything was linked to us: Putin and China, COVID and abortion bans, declining literacy rates. I don't know exactly why they became so obsessed with us. I just wanted to have a nice life and write my little extreme horror novels in peace. I guess I ended up writing in response to it, though, and I'll never know what sort of writer I would have been if I didn't live in this fucking world that forces me to write about transphobia. Maybe I'd write cool horror stories about vampires raping werewolves, ones with no subtext at all. I'm sure I wouldn't have seen the success I was lucky enough to have. I never advertised that I was a transgender woman, but I also never advertised that I was a cis woman, back then at least. People tended to assume that I was trans because I knew enough about the intimacies of trans life. My first book, TELL ME I'M WORTHLESS, was an unsubtle book but it got the job done: it was a haunted house story about a house called Brighthelm in Brighton that was haunted by the spirit of a Victorian eugenicist and his wife. It concerned a group who were called there to prove whether the house was really haunted, like the group in Richard Matheson's THE LEGEND OF HELL HOUSE. I thought it was pretty good back then, and I still do. It sold pretty well for a book that extreme (who can forget the moment where poor hapless Geri is sexually assaulted by her own reflection?), and I made a name for myself. My next book was titled EVERY MONTH THERE SHOULD BE BLOOD and was about a trans woman on the run from an abusive relationship who took shelter in a women's refuge. She never discloses that she is trans, which I suppose was an autobiographical element. Unfortunately, another girl appears who happens to be fleeing a vampiric stalker who has bitten her. Cue violence. It did just as well as my first book, and some critics said it was a little more subtle. I think they took TELL ME I'M WORTHLESS's habit of hitting the reader over the head with theme to be a negative, and maybe it was. But it was deliberate. I never wanted to write a subtle ghost story. Subtle ghost stories were all the rage back then. Most of them ended on a note of ambiguity. Mine ended on the ghosts being revealed to be real and all the characters that made it to the end burning alive, which was much more fun. I saw less backlash for the first from the growing transphobia industrial complex than I expected, but the response to the second more than made up for that. I guess that was when it really struck me, and now, looking back, that's when I should have gotten out. I didn't, and now it's too late. The borders are closed. The union flag is waving from the top of every tower, and every tower is burning.

The other day on TV I happened to catch a rerun of an old British sitcom from the early 2000s. I must have watched it at some point as a child, but I'm surprised I didn't remember it beforehand. I've tried to copy it down as best as I can below. The writer of this show went on to go noticeably insane about trans people on Twitter. He was one of the first to do so, in fact. A lot of his colleagues in the media were disturbed by it at the time, but, over the years, they all started to join him, every last one. In the episode, one character has an affair with a trans woman. When he tries to break things off with her – not for her transness, for different reasons entirely – she reacts violently. But it's before that violent comedic reaction that the most telling lines are uttered.

BRAINWYRMS

TRANS WOMAN: You don't think of me as a woman, do you?

MAN: What? Of course I do.

TRANS WOMAN: It bothers you that I used to be a man!

MAN: No! I love that you used to be a man – it's your thing. I love thinking about that operation you had.

I love thinking about that operation you had. There it is. Nearly two decades of this bullshit. Longer than that, of course. But this past two decades in particular have been bad. Things have been deteriorating. I could have left before, but I was scared, I thought I might be a coward if I did. I'm a cis woman, I am in love, I'm scared, and they love thinking about that operation I had.

When you have cut down all the trees and mined all the mountains, when you have analysed all your dreams, there will be nothing left for you to break. The earth then will be a rubbish dump, a vast trans body dismembered and devoured. The bodies of the colonists and your bodies, esteemed psychoanalysts, will be buried with the trans organs you have taken from us. But the organs that we do not have can never be buried. Our utopian organs will live on eternally. They will be the warriors storming the borders.

Paul B Preciado, *Can the Monster Speak?: Report to an Academy of Psychoanalysts,* **translated by Frank Wynne**

I was born with a dick in my brain.

Eminem, 'Insane'

The sea, if it was the sea, was the consistency of spit. It bubbled and it foamed as the waves lapped against the shore. Gently. Disconcertingly gentle all the way up the shoreline ahead. Calm as far out as the eye could see, too. It would have been easier to cope with this hell if it had been violent, like the paintings in a Catholic church. This serenity was the real torture. Just being here was adverse to their nature – it *hurt*, though the pain was not the sort they had ever felt before, certainly not of the type they usually enjoyed. But this strange country that they now traversed didn't care how they felt, they knew that. They could feel it. So they walked, both of them. Two lonely figures walking apart from one another down the beach. They didn't know where they were headed. There were hills in the distance, but Vanya couldn't look at the strange landscape for too long. When they did, they felt like they might vomit.

It was all wrong. So completely, utterly abject. The rolling hills that inflated and deflated like the external lungs of some great hidden beast. Tall rocks ... were they natural? Or were they the towers of some civilisation, hopefully long extinct but perhaps watching them through telescopes even now as they made their walk of shame and despair. There had been no sign of any intelligent life so far, which was good, possibly. In actual fact, neither Vanya nor Frankie had seen much life at all beyond the worms that sometimes wriggled across the tundra. The same sort of worm that was inside Vanya's head. When they saw one, they gave it a wide berth, although the worms did not seem interested in either of the travellers. They went about their own business. They followed their own peculiar pathways.

Behind Vanya, Frankie stumbled. Vanya heard the sound and turned to see her on her knees on the hard ground. They stopped. They didn't move to help her, but they did at least stop. They weren't that cruel.

Frankie was panting like a dog, curled up. The surface she lay on, the same one they had spent however long walking over, couldn't have been comfortable. It resembled thick black glass, and it was hot to touch. "Just like ... five minutes. I just need five minutes."

"We shouldn't wait around."

"Just five minutes, okay?"

Frankie managed to lift her head up to look at Vanya. The look in her eyes, ringed with red, took them by surprise. Her face was pale.

All Vanya could do was tell her that she looked sick, and they said it without much sympathy, if any. Frankie grimaced.

"I don't feel good, Vanya. Can you just come here please? I need ..."

"I'm fine where I am."

Frankie groaned in pain. She thumped her fist against the ground.

"What the fuck did I ever do to deserve this?"

"You hurt me," Vanya said. "You made me feel like shit."

"So did you."

Frankie was struggling to speak.

"You an-and your ... fucking gang of *rich freaks*. You ... dump me ... leave me all alone ... then you shove those *things* inside of me. This is all your fault!"

Vanya did step a little closer then. Just a little bit. Their knuckles were white. They could have punched the bitch and left her for dead. They probably should have.

"I was a fucking aimless kid when we met, Frankie. I was in an abusive housing situation, and you were my way out. You made me feel like the most important thing in the world. I didn't notice how much you were controlling me. You're a bad fucking person, and you're lucky I saved you. I felt sorry for you because of how pathetic you looked. Now you're saying that *I* hurt *you*? I should just leave you here, but I don't want to be as shit as you."

"Jesus Christ, Vanya ... I'd never f-fucking leave you."

"Well, maybe that's your problem."

She started to cry. Like a baby. Like a kid who just broke their favourite toy.

"I love you," she said. "I love you ... Sorry for how I was ... I can do better I can be ... Help me up, Vanya. Please. We c-can talk about this later."

She looked so pathetic down there. Her naked body, once an object of worship for them, now just reminded them of a large, dead fish. *Not a dead fish*, thought the very cruel part of Vanya's brain. *A beached whale*. They felt bad enough for thinking it that they gave in and walked over to help Frankie up. She didn't even say thank you.

Frankie tried to straighten up but was bent forwards by a weight that hadn't been there before. She looked down at her body and saw it. Vanya saw it too. As they looked at Frankie's stomach, a noise came from the direction of the hills. The wind, perhaps. Or something howling.

"Frankie."

They both stared, dumbfounded. Not believing her own eyes, Frankie put both of her hands on her abdomen. It was real. It was tangible. She had fantasised about this image, yes, she had fantasised about it often. The fantasy bore no relation to reality, however. She hadn't ever actually expected to see it, so seeing it made no sense. She couldn't even comprehend what she was seeing until she touched her swollen stomach, round and hard as the moon.

Inside her, something shifted. She felt whatever was in there press against her edges. Like when a baby kicked. Exactly like when a baby kicked, in fact.

"Jesus Christ, Frankie. You're ... pregnant?"

Vanya would never have believed it if they hadn't been standing where they were, in this strange, impossible nightmare place.

"I ... I know."

Frankie spoke quietly. Even as she looked down at herself, her stomach seemed to grow larger. She hadn't been pregnant a few minutes earlier, that was certain. And now here she was, nearly due to give birth.

"How?"

"The ... It came inside me," she said.

"But you don't have a fucking womb. You're a trans woman. You don't have ..."

"I know," she said. "I know."

And then her water broke, and she tumbled back down onto the glassy surface of the beach, screaming in pain. It was coming, whatever was inside of her. It was on its way. Vanya forgot how upset they'd been. They knelt beside her and clasped her hand tight in theirs. Frankie didn't look at them. *It's a fucking miracle*, she thought.

"It's a fucking miracle," Vanya said aloud, smiling. They realised what this meant. They knew what was going to happen and they couldn't stop smiling. A fucking miracle.

PART ONE

HEARTWORMS

"It's all a mess, isn't it? The one out there ... the one in here ... the one that's coming. Why is everyone so ready to think the worst is over?"

Suspiria, 2018, dir. Luca Guadagnino

1

GODLESS COCK

"Wanna get me pregnant?"

He was fucking her from behind when the question slipped out. Frankie hadn't meant to ask it, but the feeling of the dick pushing all the way up her cunt, deeper and deeper, plus the sweat dripping down her brow, and the weakness in her legs ... it had just all gotten too much. She temporarily lost her faculties, and the boundaries between thought and speech blurred. She had been fantasising that his cock would (could!) knock her up, and then, in the midst of the fantasy, she spoke it aloud. For a moment she thought he might not have heard, or, thick as he was, maybe he wouldn't get what she was on about. But no. He was a himbo but not *that* much of a himbo. Oh well, she thought. If he really was as stupid as she expected, fucking him would probably have been breaking some kind of power-imbalance law. It might have somehow constituted statutory rape. His pounding slowed and stopped. She felt his dick soften a little in her cunt, and then he pulled himself out with a nice, wet sound. At least that was a satisfying noise. She always enjoyed hearing it.

"What did you just ask me?"

Fuck.

"Ignore me," she said. "I didn't mean to say that."

She was still staring right at the wall. *Just go back to fucking me just go back to fucking me please please please I was so close I was so close …*

"Well why did you say it then?"

"I was … I was just thinking about it."

He didn't say anything, so she sat up and turned to him. "Are you going to keep fucking me?"

That didn't seem to be on the cards. He stood there, dick drooping down. His legs were far enough apart and his shoulders broad enough that his whole stance was honestly very funny, and if she wasn't so fucking embarrassed, she would have laughed at him, even if that didn't seem like something he'd get off on. He looked at her cunt like it had suddenly grown teeth. *Fuck you and your big mouth, Frankie.* There were people who would get it and people who wouldn't, and this guy was firmly in the latter category, whatever his name was. He called himself The Stallion. His IQ was probably slightly below that of his namesake, but his dick made up for that.

"I thought you were trans," he said. It wasn't an answer to her question. Well, fuck her for wanting to cum.

"I am, obviously. Can't you tell?"

This only made him more confused, and she knew she had put him in a difficult position with the question. There was no good answer. If he said yes, then he was saying she didn't pass. If he said no, then he would be lying. Outside the room she could hear and feel the music. Out there it probably didn't feel quite as awkward as in here. The big, dumb, horse-like man stood there with his mouth opening and closing, and all the while his cock drooped lower and lower.

"I have an impregnation fetish." No answer still. "Oh come on dude. Half the twinks here talk about wanting to be bred, and not in a bug-chaser way."

"Man sorry, I just … I'm not into that," he said. "Sorry."

She watched him pull up his chaps and thump out of the room. When he was pulling the door shut behind him, she called out to him, "We could have made a beautiful baby!"

Her cunt throbbed when she pulled herself up off the bench. There was still lube between her pussy lips. She couldn't get wet, but it was the next best thing, and if she was fucking a fag like the Stallion it was unlikely he'd know the difference. It would probably be the only cunt he'd see all year. She pulled her thong up. *Just like Mama always said, pull up your thong and button your shirt, don't dawdle.* Before she left the private room, she was courteous enough to wipe off the bench a little. There was a sign on the door with a little stick-man gimp wiping down a dildo with the instruction *please leave the room clean and tidy*. Fucking cocksucker. Damn it, she needed to cum tonight! She also needed a drink and a smoke and maybe a bump, but most of all she needed to get off. She hadn't had sex in a week. Practically a year, practically a cobwebs situation. Practically a Virgin Mary, unfortunately without the miracle pregnancy. Would it be hot to get knocked up by God? The thing that made it sexy was someone cream-pieing her and getting her pregnant. Just a random pregnancy out of the blue would mean missing the best bit. It would still be hot knowing it happened, though. She could probably work with it, if God ever decided she was the right Mum for the second coming.

Through the door the music went from a background drone to unbearably loud, at least in her right ear. In her left ear it was dulled, as if she was hearing it play through deep water. The dancefloor was a chaotic pile of people dressed for every kink under the sun, although a lot of the cis girlies had opted for what Frankie suspected was Ann Summers sale lingerie. *Bless them. They don't know any better!* Their boyfriends had clearly struggled with what to wear. A few of them wore their girlfriends' lingerie too. *Bless them*, she thought again, imagining herself as Mother Mary hovering in the air above the mess of them, bestowing golden-crowned hearts upon them. Benevolent was she. Not the type of girl with a counter of how many eggs she'd cracked in her Twitter bio or anything. She was just benevolent, that was all. *They clamoured at her perfect feet (natural size five), and she rained down kisses on their cheeks. And when they awoke the next day, they found themselves changed and renewed and self-aware, they found they had enjoyed wearing their girlfriends' lingerie and would like to do it again sometime etc, etc, etc.*

Lula was dancing with a group of girls. She wore absurdly steep heels and a full pink latex bodysuit. She looked gorgeous, but Frankie knew that inside the latex she must have been drenched in sweat. She could probably feel the sweat squelching against her as she thrust her ass back and forth in time to the music. Frankie waved to her, but Lula didn't see. She stood on the edge of the dancefloor trying to decide if she should go over or not, and if not, where else she could go. The Stallion was on the other side of the dancefloor leaning against the bar and talking to somebody else already, though she couldn't quite see who. *What a slut!*

In front of the throng of dancers was a stage. To one side, a serious-looking DJ bent over their decks, but anybody looking in that direction wasn't looking at them, they were looking at the guy on the ropes. Above a raised platform, attended by two anonymous people in black, a man swung from the ceiling. Ropes were tied around his ankles, his knees, his wrists and his torso. He was on his back; his shoulders and head hung low and upside down, staring right back at the audience. His cock was hard, it lanced skywards. Hard to tell given that he was upside down, but he wasn't really her type. The guy looked more like a roadie in the eighties than some kink god. But it was hot to see someone so vulnerable, so nakedly in the hands of those around them. Two trans girls she didn't know were talking about him as they walked past her. One was saying she thought the suspension thing was fun, but it was a little weak to just tie the ropes; she much preferred it when people used hooks through the flesh. The other girl agreed, but pointed out that obviously the venue couldn't really get away with that. It would be overwhelming, surely, to be elevated off the ground, blood rushing to the head ... The man didn't look overwhelmed, but he didn't look orgasmic either. His face was stone. All part of the performance, she guessed.

She circled the dancefloor like a shark, eyes scanning everybody she passed for someone she could dazzle into fucking her. When she made it to the bar, she stood and waited for attention. It wasn't long before a short, pale guy wearing a maid dress sidled up to her, nervousness practically dripping down his forehead. He was good to get a drink out of but nothing more. She made him buy her a triple before abandoning him, which was fine – he'd probably have a wank thinking about it later. He might have just tried to confess that sometimes he didn't know if he was a man to her, and it would be *agony*. She lost him easily and ducked out into the smoking area where the air was so much cooler.

Jade was talking to some girls, smoking fags with them. The smoking area was raised a little above street level for privacy, but from it you could see the beach and the black ocean, and there were fires on the beach too, groups of unhoused men huddling together.

"Hi babe," said Jade, beckoning her over. "Fag?"

"Just can't pass up the opportunity, that's all." Frankie didn't smoke much anymore, but she took two from the box and lit one with Jade's offered lighter.

"Having fun?" asked Jade.

"The suspended guy is cool. The music … eh, I could take it or leave it. I had some great sex with this fucking stud of a guy, but he couldn't cum so he left."

"What? Did he try to make you cum?"

"Not really."

"Asshole!" Jade nudged her friend. "This guy didn't even *try* to make her cum!"

"That sucks," said the girl. Frankie had seen the girl around but didn't know her name and didn't really care to know. She hoped that the Stallion hadn't come out here as well. She didn't want him correcting her version of the story. The first cigarette finished too quickly so she lit the second, but a few puffs in her stomach started to cramp, so she gave it up and crushed it under her boot. Jade scowled.

"You just wasted a fag."

Frankie flashed her most winning smile.

"Are you okay?" asked Jade again.

"I'm fine." The cramp in her abdomen hurt.

"I just know you're still new to this sort of thing …"

"I'm fine."

"Are you sure?"

Frankie bit her lip. "Do you think I'm sensitive, Jade?" Jade opened her mouth and closed it again. She looked like a fish. "Do you think I'm *over*sensitive?"

"God, Frankie, why do you have to be like this? Every time anyone shows they care about you, you act like it's a personal *fucking* insult."

"Well, if you're going to patronise me then, yes, I will take it as a fucking insult. Look, you and Lula are ever going to understand it, and I'd rather you didn't try."

Jade's friends were still standing there, looking at each other and shifting awkwardly. They weren't sure what to do. Jade just rolled her eyes. Tired of this shit happening all the time.

"You're not the only girl to ever have trauma, Frankie." But Frankie had already turned to head back inside.

There was a crowd of people coming through the door into the smoking area and she barged right through them. Sometimes, when things were bad, she saw everybody's faces as the same face, a face that she was unable to recall when lucid, but that loomed at her from the dark, stared down at her from the windows of houses she passed, pinched cat's arse mouth and dry sandy hair and those blue, blue eyes. It was fine. Everything was fine. She wasn't here, why would she be?

It would be so easy for someone to take out everyone in this club. If people had guns here, like they did in America, they could just spray into the crowd. If you got nerve gas you could release it into the air conditioning, which was working overtime in the sweaty hell of the dancefloor. It was a queer kink club. There had to be a lot of people out there who wanted all these people dead, all the catgirls and the leather daddies and the bodies encased in coffins of rubber. On a better night, it might have been life-affirming: so many people from so many corners of the community together and dancing as one, so close they might as well have been one colossal, beautiful mass of living, breathing, fucking flesh. It was a shit night, though. She was in a shit mood. All Jade's fault, bringing up the fucking bombing when they were out clubbing. How would she like it if Frankie brought up that time she got spiked by a guy, or that time she got fucking gang-raped? *Yeah, thought not.* Lula was dancing with a group of fags right in her eyeline, but she wanted to speak to her about as much as she wanted to speak to Jade. They'd probably talk about this shit later. They probably had intense discussions about whether to hold an intervention.

Somehow, rope guy had twisted onto his front. His long hair now covered his face, but through it she could just about see his eyes flashing in the lights. He held poses for such long stretches of time that he really might as well have been sculpture. Maybe he was hot, she thought. If she'd seen him without the ropes, she wouldn't have cared, but ... a guy who was so into being so open ... it was kind of cute. It made him cuter, at least. There were a lot of *cute* people in this club. Boys in their lingerie and girls in their lingerie. *I'm not here. Nobody can see me. I am fading.* She was lightheaded but she didn't want to head back outside, and her stomach hurt, but she didn't think she was going to throw up.

Coke would help, probably. Coke would drag her back down to earth. That was the sort of thing a cokehead thought right before snorting some, but she wasn't a cokehead, she didn't have a habit, even if she took it every other weekend. It was every *other* weekend, after all. Every weekend and maybe there'd be a problem, maybe the girls would be justified in their little intervention scheme. She didn't really know that was what they wanted, but she got the general idea of how they viewed her. They probably hoovered more lines than she ever had! All this thinking about coke got to her. It was what she needed, clearly, or else she wouldn't be thinking about it so much. But just when she turned towards the toilets with the intention of finding some twink to give her a bump, she saw Vanya for the first time.

Everything else stopped, every other dancer, grotesque visage, every speck of dust in the air: they all slowed to a crawl and a spotlight fell on Vanya. They might as well have had a halo. They were the only thing that had ever been, the only thing that could ever be: *Vanya, light of my life, fire of my loins. My sin, my soul. Van-ya: the tip of the tongue taking a trip of two skips down the palate to tap on the teeth. Van. Ya. Petit little Polish elf. Baby. Daddy. Puppy. Good girl, good boy. Short king.*

Vanya hadn't seen her. Their face was turned towards the man tangled in his ropes, deathly still even if time hadn't just stopped. Frankie knew the moment she saw them that she needed them with every part of herself. She couldn't have said why. Call it gut instinct, call it love at first sight. They leaned against a wall, face turned to the side. In one hand they held a drink. Nobody else around them. Completely alone. Frankie wondered for just a moment if anybody else could even see them. She approached them cautiously, as one might an injured fawn, but her resolve was tested when they noticed her. They turned, they looked. The look in their eyes. She thought she might piss herself.

"Hi there," they said. "Have we met before?"

"I don't think so, no. I feel like I'd remember if we had."

"Oh ... was there something you wanted?"

"No, no," she said, blushing like a teenager with a crush. "I just saw you and thought *wow*, so I came over to say 'hi'."

Vanya looked confused for a moment, as if the possibility Frankie was hitting on them just hadn't entered their mind at all, which seemed ridiculous given that they were at a fetish club. But who was Frankie to judge. It's easy to get lost in the moment, easy to forget that you're even perceivable to others. Everyone around them started to become real again. They sped up, and they had the correct faces. Everything was fine, nothing was fucked up at all – in fact it was more than fine because fuck, the way Vanya looked up at her, how wide their eyes were. Innocent, which was ridiculous because, again, they were at a fetish club. They smiled. They told Frankie that she was pretty. Frankie blushed like a schoolgirl.

"Oh shh," said Frankie. "You're so fucking cute. Have you seen yourself?"

They chuckled. "You're a charmer. I'm Vanya, by the way."

"That's a nice name," she said.

"Is it? I've been thinking about changing it."

"I'm Frankie."

"Hi Frankie," they replied. "So, I don't want to be too forward, but I might as well ask, given where we are. What is it that gets you off?"

2

WHAT HAPPENED BY HILLARY RODHAM CLINTON

Six months and eight days earlier.

You've hurt your head, somehow. Somehow you have hurt your head. Yes, you're right. My head does hurt. *Your eyes are closed. I think. Do you have eyes?* I think that I have eyes. *You should open them, then.* Well. I don't want to. *You'll have to eventually.* Will I? *Yes. Listen for a moment now.* Hmm. Okay ... *What do you hear?* Well, on my right I can hear a beeping. It happens every second or so. *On your left?* I can hear the same beeping. *But?* But its quieter. *What does this tell you?* The source of the beeping is on my right. *Maybe.* What are you suggesting? *Nothing, nothing. Do you want to open your eyes?* No. *What do you want to do?* I don't know. I hurt. My body hurts. I suppose

31

that means I have a body, which is a pity. *It is.* Can I die? *Well, you're a human so yes you are capable of death.* I meant, can I die now? *Do you mean, is it a risk to you?* No, I mean that I think I'd like it if I died. *Why?* I can't remember. *Well, regardless. No, it's my job to keep you alive.* Ugh! *Look, I know you don't like that. But it's just a psychological thing. It's what I do.* Can I beat you? *No.* How did I get here? *There was a thing. I'm not sure. I know about as much as you know, given that I am a natural part of your brain and that you are not having a conversation with another person, just with yourself.* Stupid twist. *It's not a twist, it's just reality.* I don't like reality. *Does anyone?* I can't remember being a kid. I can't … Maybe I was never a kid. *You were.* Why can't I remember being a child then? If I was a child, then how come I don't remember it? *Everybody is a child at least once.* I don't believe you … I don't. If I'd been a child, I think I would remember. Real people were kids once. They can remember being kids. They can remember their parents. *Not everyone.* Shut up. *I'm trying to be reasonable. I'm trying to stop you from dying.* Fuck off. *Do you remember what happened?* I don't want to. *Do you remember what the remains of her looked like?* Get the fuck out of my head. *It's not nice. Not nice. But you need to know. That's the thread that pulls you back towards the sun.* I hate the sun, it's too hot, it's getting hotter every year. *You think that often. That's good. There's the thread. There's the tug and the pull of the rope around you.* Fuck off. Fuck off. Fuck off and leave me alone.

Sigh. Well, there's no point in my being here if you're going to be like that.

Who are you anyway? Hello?

Hello? Ah, fuck. Come back. I'm sorry. I didn't mean to ... I didn't mean to do that.

There was no answer. She drifted back off to sleep, and a little while later she awoke to a brightness surrounding her. It wasn't the sun – it was a hospital room. She thought hospital rooms were usually white for some reason; this one was an ugly light blue colour, with some green lino flooring. A male nurse was, at the moment she opened her eyes, passing by the end of her bed. He definitely saw her, but he said nothing.

"Hello?" she said to him, but he had already vanished.

There were flowers on her bedside table, and the sun came through the strip blinds in segmented bars of yellow light. The air smelled of something like floor cleaner. There was another body in a bed next to hers, but she could only see the faint shadow of it behind the curtain they'd put around it. It moved a little. Nobody had put a curtain around her. Her head spun. The beeping was still louder in one ear than in the other, and the sheer brightness of everything made her eyes and her skull throb.

She'd been lying there for a while before Lula and Jade appeared at her bedside. They had to stop themselves from hugging her too hard. She told them they didn't have to worry about breaking her, she wasn't made of glass. Neither of them made any comment about that. They asked her if she remembered what happened. "No", she said. "I can't remember a thing." She knew who they were, which was good. She knew that she was Frankie, and that she was a woman, which was good. But that was all there was in her head right then. Jade and Lula looked at each other, and then Jade made to speak. She told Frankie what had happened, slowly and carefully, so as not to overwhelm her.

She, Frankie, had been the victim of a terrorist attack. *Really?* It sounded like the sort of thing that happened to somebody else, somebody on the news. She had been at work. *Where did I work?* A GIC, apparently. For children. *Oh ...* She was a trans woman. She remembered that now. She thought she was just a regular, not-trans woman. She didn't have a dick, that was nice to remember. For a moment, upon remembering her transness, she had thought she could feel it, but it was just an awkward fold in the hospital gown.

She'd been finishing work when a woman walked in, obviously agitated. This happened sometimes: parents of children who were in the early stages of transitioning came in with anxieties or questions. Obviously, by that point, people were aware that there was a growing threat, although the only clinics to have ever faced violence were in America, and even then, there had only been threats. So yeah, Frankie should have been more aware. She wasn't, and neither was her nice cis co-worker, Tabi. They didn't really pay the woman much mind at all. Maybe if Frankie had properly looked at her, she would have been able to actually describe her face. She might have even seen the fear and the resolve in the way she looked around the clinic from her vantage point on one of the waiting room chairs. It was the end of the day. They couldn't be bothered.

The woman sat there for five minutes before she got up and left. A minute after she left, Tabi noticed that she had left her rucksack behind, under the chair. When Tabi picked it up, the bomb inside exploded. She was killed right away, the lucky bitch. Cis girls are always spared the worst of the pain.

Now she'd been told this story, Frankie felt like she could remember it. She even felt like she could see the images in her head, but she didn't know if they bore any relation to reality, or if she had just conjured them to illustrate the story being told. Still, the image was there: Tabi, thrown against the wall by the explosion, head torn apart. Frankie had been sitting behind her desk, shielded from most of the blast. Medically, she was considered more or less intact; there were a lot of bruises of course, and damage to her hearing. That was why the heart monitor sounded so unbalanced, then. But the *damage* to her mind was far more significant, as she would soon find out. The self-harm, the bingeing, the guilt, all of that came later, but the depression was already there in her hospital bed with her.

After the explosion, she'd shuffled out into the street, dazed and staring at the faces of people who'd come over to see what that noise had been. She couldn't understand why they were looking at her. She couldn't understand what they wanted her to say. The paramedics came and wrapped her in one of those shining, silvery foil blankets. A picture of her there, sitting on the curb, had gone viral on Twitter. After that she collapsed, and they took her to the hospital.

Frankie felt exhausted. After Jade had finished her story, she and Lula made their excuses and left her there to rest, promising they would be back. Others would come soon. Cops, journalists. *Parasitic life-forms.*

Had her stepparents seen that picture of her? And if so, had they recognised her? That was the last thought she had before she fell asleep again; it was a disquieting thought. She didn't want to see her family. She didn't want sympathy from them, to hear their worries and their regrets and all their reasonable concerns about her world. It would be fine, probably. They probably didn't care about her that much. They probably couldn't remember what she looked like. Consciousness faded once again. She slept for an entire day, but the sleep was not peaceful: it was riddled with bad dreams in which something large and unseen was stalking her across a wide, flat plain. There was no escape, no place of safety, and no way of knowing what it was. However fast she ran, however quietly she crept, it knew where she was, and it was getting closer. *It's the future*, she thought as she tried to wake herself up. *The thing that's hunting me is the future.*

3

COTTAGECORE

" ... What is it that gets you off?"

Vanya's big eyes could have been unsettling, and they would have been if Frankie wasn't so entranced by them. They stared right into her eyes as they asked her, and inched closer, just a little. It disarmed her. She should be the one in control. Why wasn't she the one in control? It pissed her off, and she moved closer too. But when she answered the question, she knew she sounded weak.

"Just stuff, you know. I'm fairly new to the scene. I'm still exploring."

Just stuff? She wanted to run away. She wanted to smash her head into the wall.

She was twenty-eight. She knew *exactly* what she liked, but there was no way she was about to open with "I have an impregnation fetish" to someone who was presumably not in possession of a cock. Of course, Frankie didn't have a womb, but it made it more viable if at least one person involved in the sex had one of the parts needed for impregnation to happen.

"Something tells me you're playing coy, Frankie ... Well, I can play along with that. *I* like being choked and spanked and fucked hard. I like ... stuff when I'm asleep. Um ... I like rape play and age play, you know," said Vanya. Their face was so cute. It seemed so wrong saying these things. *I like rape.*

She felt a twinge of excitement in her cunt. She thought about holding Vanya down, pushing their face in a puddle in an alleyway someplace they couldn't be heard. The sort of thing she never dreamed of trying because of all the effort of safewords and aftercare, parts of kink she could never be fucked with. And they'd like it. They'd want more. She was out of her depth. This wasn't her shit at all.

"I'd never have guessed," she purred, touching one finger to their shoulder. "You look so young and innocent. How do you know about all these things?"

"I suppose I am young. But I'm mature for my age. So, I was honest with you ... Come on, tell me what you're actually into!"

Frankie lied to cis men all the time. To some of them, she elected to tell a selective truth and avoided disclosing her transgender status, something she knew would get her branded as a rapist by some people online, and even by some Members of Parliament. But it didn't matter, they liked her pussy just as much as any pussy they'd ever had. Sometimes they liked it more. Often, they liked it more. Other guys, the ones who were fags, chasers, eggs, or just plain transamorous men, she told the truth to, but she would lie about other things. If they asked what her ethnicity was, she might say Italian or Jewish. She told them she transitioned at age twelve. It was easier to lie to men, it was fun, and it was safer that they didn't know too much about you. It was easy to lie to Vanya, too, but she wished it hadn't been.

"I like to be dominant," she said. "And everything that entails. I like to be in control."

"Oh?" Vanya was setting her up, which irked her. It went against the point of domination, surely, for someone to prompt you to tell them what to do. Vanya was so cute, perhaps the cutest thing in the fucking world, but God were they hard work already. She needed to piss, she needed some coke or something. Perhaps some quiet so they could talk properly would do good.

She needed a piss.

The idea came to her. She smiled like the Cheshire Cat and told Vanya what to do.

∼

By the time Frankie realised that she'd never asked for Vanya's pronouns, the two of them were in the bathroom, and Vanya was knelt on the tiled floor, no matter how wet it was, with their face pressed between her thighs.

"She and they," Vanya said. They looked up at her as they said it. There was lube all across their face; it looked like highlighter. Frankie had positioned herself on the toilet. There was a playroom just for this sort of thing, but Frankie had told Vanya, quite firmly, that they were going to find a stall in the women's loos. That was part of the fun: people walking past, going to shit or piss or do drugs or cry in one of the other stalls, might see Vanya's legs kneeling under the door, or they might hear Frankie's soft moans. People were all around, separated only by plywood. That was better than actually being watched sometimes. Inconveniencing others was fun.

She could see them both reflected in the puddles on the floor. Two peculiar shapes moving together, shivering with the occasional ripple. An entire alternate world reflected there. A world of piss and spilled alcohol, inhabited by ghosts.

Vanya's mouth on her thighs. Vanya's tongue circling her clit. When she fucked trans girls they always commented on her cunt, and many asked her who her surgeon was. Some were envious or jealous, some had not yet had the operation, some were simply curious. It was a good cunt, she knew. But she had fucked too many cisgender men recently, that was clear: being eaten out by someone who knew what they were doing made her gasp for the stale toilet air and grasp the bars on the side of the accessible cubical until her knuckles were white. How were they *this* experienced this young? *God, don't think about that. Think about how good it feels.*

Someone thumped on the door with their fist. "There's playrooms for a reason!" said a voice.

"Fuck off," said Frankie, trying her best not to moan. "I'm just … pissing!"

Then, under her breath, she told Vanya that if they made a sound, they'd be very sorry.

Footsteps moved away again. She heard a grumpy sigh.

"I guess if I told that person I was pissing," said Frankie, "then I need to piss."

Vanya shut their eyes and opened up their mouth, and Frankie understood that they were on the same wavelength. Their mouth was a beautifully crafted ivory urinal. Bespoke. *You were made for me, Vanya*, she thought, as she relaxed her muscles and shuffled forwards to get into position. *You're all mine.* She'd pissed on a few men, once for money. It was hard to describe what was fun about it. In a way, it was easier to understand what was hot about being pissed on – that was so degrading, so filthy. But pissing on someone ... The pisser is dominant, but pissing itself is a moment of pure vulnerability. It's about loss of control. The power dynamics were more complicated than they appeared to outsiders.

She could feel it coming, now.

"Oh God," she said, and looked down as urine flushed out of her, all over Vanya's face. Most of it flowed into their mouth, but Frankie wasn't an expert markswoman. It splashed on their cheeks, on their nose. Droplets got in their hair.

"Drink it up you fucking slut," she said.

Vanya swallowed once she had finished, and then opened their eyes up to look into her face. Frankie had never felt this close to anybody. This was the intimacy people talked about, the thing she had always considered purely theoretical.

Vanya wiped their mouth with the back of their hand and then licked it clean.

"Good boy."

"I try my best to look good for you, Mummy."

When they left, she felt a pang of guilt about taking up space in the disabled toilet. She could imagine the event organisers posting tomorrow on social media, something along the lines of *We are aware some people decided to use the accessible toilets for play, and are very disappointed by this. We would have hoped that those who came here read our rules carefully and understood that we don't allow ableist behaviour.* They hurried out, trying not to meet anyone's eye. Vanya had wiped their mouth but some of her piss still glittered on their cheeks, even when they got into the taxi home together. The whole way home, Frankie touched Vanya's cunt, trying and probably failing to be subtle. The driver could definitely see; he wasn't an idiot. Vanya was bad at keeping quiet. They'd be punished for that. But oh well, the poor guy had probably had a long night driving people to and from clubs, so they might as well give him a bit of a show.

4

REASONABLE CONCERNS

'The gender clinic bomber is repulsive, but that doesn't mean we should discount her fears', by Karen Anson. Written for *The Observer*'s "Opinion" section.

I already know people will share this piece and claim that I am a terrorist sympathiser based on the title alone, without ever reading further. I've made peace with that. People on Twitter and Facebook are averse to any kind of real intellectual engagement, and their "opinions" are an echo chamber. So, sure. I sympathise with the person who planted a bomb at the gender clinic. That doesn't mean I am a terrorist sympathiser because that person is not necessarily a terrorist – they are a person who, misguidedly, felt they only had one course of action to stop what they perceived as a rising threat. I say "they", but we know this person was a woman and a mother. We do not know who she is yet, but someone claiming to be her, via an anonymous account on a forum, posted an outline of why she did it. She was a mother anxious about what was happening to her daughter. Her daughter had been, in her words, radicalised, which, in turn, caused her to be radicalised too. She wanted to stop the tide that was spreading, causing her daughter to hate her body and want to, in her words, "mutilate herself". Now, the way she went about that was horrible. There are proper channels for this. But, and this is heavy to admit, especially to myself, I sympathise with the fact that she felt she had been failed by those proper channels.

We live in a world where women with these anxieties are increasingly demonised. Claire Greenaway, a professor of philosophy at Oxford, recently posted an image on Twitter of the vandalism done to her office the day after she published a piece concerning her worries about transgender individuals participating in women's rowing. Just for speaking her mind, her place of work was attacked, graffitied, and her personhood smeared. And this is the case all over. Every time a woman dares speak on this topic, the same thing happens. I myself have had people call the offices of the paper where I work, asking for me to be fired, sometimes threatening me with physical violence. People have threatened the publisher that I have a deal with. They have called in (fake) bomb threats against them. I have even been threatened personally with murder, assault and rape. I'm sure this will happen again once people read this piece, or, more accurately, once they read the headline to this piece. They won't get far enough to see these words, or bother to use the part of their brain that is *supposed* to be for critical thinking.

To put it simply: the climate around this debate has reached the point where a woman felt her only course of action was to plant a bomb. That is, if nothing else, a serious indictment of the way this conversation has gone. Women should feel safe to express their thoughts and feelings, without being pushed to extremist actions. I have attended meetings of women trying to seriously discuss the topic, only to find crowds of people attempting to intimidate us into silence. The police, in that instance, were no help at all, and did not act as allies to women. They just stood and watched. And thinking back to that moment? Yes, it felt hopeless. It felt like I had no voice at all.

The instincts of a mother are powerful and innate. There's the old story about mothers finding themselves suddenly able to lift cars to save their children. I think, if you asked any mother, they would proudly say they would kill for their child. Now, planting a bomb is a whole different thing ... but that instinct? That is the instinct of a mother, resorting to violence because she sees it as the only way she can ensure the protection of her child. And if you want my honest opinion? This won't be the last time this happens, unless the climate around the debate changes. We have to let people speak their mind without silencing them, or more people will die. It is inevitable. I don't want it to happen. I am trying to prevent more tragedies such as the one we saw last month (although, of course, people will screenshot this out of context and say that I *do* want more attacks like this. Long live the Twitter trolls, I guess.).

I want everybody to feel safe. I want trans individuals to feel safe and secure, and I want women, I want mothers, to feel safe and secure. This is not, currently, the situation, and I don't know for certain how we should get there. Trans people will claim that they are being murdered but, overwhelmingly, it is not women who do the murdering: it is men. Men are our common enemy, yet we fight among ourselves, smearing the other side as "transphobic", or "not real feminists".

So, hear this. Let this be a warning, a plea for sanity and rationality. Keep the debate open, and keep speech free, or we are in danger of seeing more and more of this violence.

@unionsalabs: what the fuck is this. you are a disgusting terrorist sympathiser, and the fact that this was published in a national newspaper is horrifying

@xxterrichromozone: THank you Karen for posting what we are all thinking but are too afraid to say.

@feministallyfather34: Every day I worry that my daughter will cme home and tell me she wants to wear a "binder" and defile her beautiful breasts.

@holeincorporated: hey karen how about i fucking bomb your workplace, then try and justify it [This account was deleted by Twitter for violating their TOS]

@verminturnin: a woman DIED holy shit

5

WHIPPING GIRL

Frankie arrived at her desk four minutes after she was supposed to, visibly shaking and sure that the sweat on her brow and the circles under her eyes were obvious to absolutely everyone else in the office. *Stupid fucking bitch taking a shift on a Sunday.* A surreptitious glance around gave her some comfort, though: everyone else looked hungover as fuck as well. Even her manager, Kevin, who had watched her late entrance like a hawk watching the movements of a sparrow through a clear sky, looked a little pale. He probably stayed up too late playing *CS:GO* or something, though. At least she could say she pissed on a cute bitch's face.

Her desktop computer roared into ancient life. Hot air tumbled out of the vents in its sides. It was like some old, decrepit monster, breathing despite how broken it was. The screen sputtered on. This shit was all ancient. They were expected to meet astronomical targets every day on the sort of computers she'd used at secondary school. The room was an ambient soundscape of desktop fans, sighs, and coughs. The ambience always got on her nerves. Some people listened to ambient sounds to relax, but it just made her mind wander into worse and worse places. She put in her earphones.

Kevin was watching her. She resisted the urge to look up at him. Instead, her eyes stayed fixed to the screen even though the blue light stung her retinas. She turned the brightness down quickly until it hurt less. She didn't need another fucking migraine breaking through today, although she could feel one there, waiting around in the back of her head, looming over her. Had she packed her painkillers? It wasn't possible to check now, not with Kevin's eyes on her. Wait and see, wait until later.

~

While the program was still booting up, on the other end of Frankie's morning commute, Vanya was stirring in Frankie's bed. They found the note she had left on the bedside table next to their phone, which she had plugged in to charge: "Coffee in top cupboard along w sugar. Oat milk in fridge. Here's my number: _____. Can we see each other again?" Vanya looked at the note, and then at Frankie's ceiling, before running to what they guessed was the bathroom and vomiting in the sink. *Christ, what did you do, Vanya? Where have you ended up now? What have you put inside yourself? Texts on your*

*phone, missed calls and voicemails, all from Gaz, screaming at you
asking where you were, why you didn't tell him, how dare you not
inform him, do you think you're better than him ... throw up some
more. He'd cool off, soon. You hoped he would anyway because
despite the hangover you're already horny and you want what only
Gaz can give to you. Pathetic slut. You're the lowest of the fucking
low. You're nothing, you're shit. You should drink Frankie's toilet
water. You shouldn't be allowed coffee.* On and on like that.

~

Frankie felt sick and, given the content of her work, she
probably would *be* sick before the day was done. A little digital
pinwheel span in the centre of the screen. It spun for about a
minute, and then, quite suddenly, the first of today's countless
posts appeared. The loading always took a long enough time
that it was a surprise, and a disappointment, when it actually
finished.

Every day, people posted things on social media. Every
day, a high percentage of those things could be considered
abusive, violent, threatening, sexually explicit, or illegal.
Of that very high percentage, a very small percentage was
reported. A very small percentage of a very high percentage
of posts is an impossibly large number, however small the
percentage. The internet was vast. Trying to consider that
vastness could induce pain in the mind of a person. She saw
so much shit every day. For every five hundred rape threats,
there was a video of a beheading or the cartel killing of a

woman or leaked photographs of a celebrity suicide. Thank fuck the computers were so old. If this shit loaded up any faster than it did, then her brain would have fully broken on the first day of working here.

It was her job to decide if something reported to her broke the website's guidelines. Very occasionally, something more serious, potentially illegal, could be referred elsewhere in the system, although she suspected nothing ever happened with those referrals. Today's first post was relatively gentle, thank fuck. You don't want to start the day off confronted with some kiddie porn. Luckily this was just some skinnygirl femcel bullshit: *Things were better in the early 2000s when everyone knew SKINNY was BETTER. Now people have gotten far too comfortable being fat lazy fucks. Here's how to get skinny in TEN easy steps* ... Accompanying those words and the subsequent thread was a picture of a thin white girl in a bikini. Her skin was almost translucent. Touch her and your fingers would probably pass right through into her insides, her skin just a layer of mist or a hologram.

The scared-animal look on the girl's face wasn't so far from a look Vanya had worn at points last night, and the girl's ribcage, defined and contoured like mountains from above, was very much like Vanya's. She had been scared of breaking them into pieces, but that hadn't stopped her from flogging their bony arse with her faux-leather whip until it was criss-crossed all over with strips of red-raw flesh. *Harder! Harder! Mummy I need you to do it harder or I'll misbehave again ... Mummy!* The girl on the screen with the thin skin and the big eyes was screaming that too. Everybody was always screaming it. Vanya had stood up to a lot of punishment, more than she imagined someone their size and age could take. The thin girl disappeared; Frankie sent her away. She violated the TOS.

~

"I'm sorry," they said. "I really am, Gaz. I was just having fun, it wasn't anything serious, I just wanted to fuck someone ... Please don't be mad at me..."

There was silence on the other end of the line. Vanya lay curled up on Frankie's bathroom floor. Their phone lay on the tiles right in front of their face, speaker on.

"Gaz? Are you there?"

More silence.

"Daddy?"

"I'm here, baby."

"Please, please forgive me ..." They started to sob and shake so much that it was hard for them to say anything more.

"Of course I'll forgive you," said the posh voice on the phone. "I was just a little upset that you didn't tell me where you were. Next time, just tell me where you are, and everything will be okay."

They started to breathe a little slower.

"Are you sure?"

"Of course I'm sure. But you will need to do due penance."

Vanya knew what he meant. It made their blood run cold, but it made their cunt throb, too. *You're scared. You don't want to go back there, you don't want to know what he means by that. Just stay here in Frankie's bed, clean her flat, cook her dinner and be here when she gets back to eat her pussy when she tells you to eat it. Hide here. Hide in her fucking wardrobe or something, you stupid slut. Just don't go back there, you don't have to endure it, but you want to endure it, you want what's coming to you, that's how you know you're sick, that's how you know there's no saving you no redemption no grace you are the drowned rat in the drain in the downward spiral you'll go to hell when you eventually die drugged out in some basement somewhere with nobody to mourn you...*

The air was warm enough outside that their tears dried quickly in the gentle breeze. They caught a look at themselves in the window of a parked car. Dark circles, greasy hair, pale skin, bruised thighs ... They snapped a selfie and sent it to the number Frankie had left.

Love how punished I look. Hope to see you again. Vanya x

~

Frankie genuinely didn't expect to receive that text, let alone the accompanying selfie. Last night had been so hot, but for whatever reason she thought it might be a one-time thing. It would have been easier. Vanya was bad news; she wasn't too stupid to realise that. They were young, although she didn't know how young. They looked like they might have some kind of eating disorder. She didn't know where their limits were, or even if they had any. So, maybe she'd been hoping that they might just not message. Then she would have had an excuse to move on. Now, with this text and this selfie, a door had opened, a door that every instinct told her was dangerous. Obviously she was going to walk through it, into the dark beyond.

Frankie didn't see the text until lunchtime, by which point she had trawled through so many reported posts that they seemed to blur into one great post – the *uberpöst*. A post that was hateful in every possible way: racist, transphobic, misogynistic, homophobic, ableist all at once. The energy of some old Eminem song distilled into a single post. This post didn't exist, it was the invention of her hungover mind. But it was an interesting thought experiment. Should this post exist, would it negate the existence of every other abusive post online? Her job would certainly be easier, but it would also mean she'd have no more work to do here. They'd probably let her go with a joyful mass email. *Well done everyone. That was the only nasty post. Go outside and enjoy the flowers!*

In the Pret closest to her work, she sat next to her co-worker, staring down at the message from Vanya. They came here a lot, generally if they both happened to be working. Neither had any particular love for Pret; its coffee tasted, to Frankie, like McDonald's coffee with a fancier cup, and the sandwiches always looked like they had been sat on at some point between the kitchen and her table. She didn't want to eat the egg and cress sandwich, but she knew she should. It would be worse not eating. There's nothing worse than dry retching, nothing on earth.

Wolf, her colleague, broke the silence. She insisted that everybody call her that, and some people went along with it. Others didn't call her anything at all.

"Who you texting?"

"Hook-up from last night."

"Girl?"

Frankie shrugged. "I'm tired."

"Same."

"I fucking hate this job."

"I saw someone post a picture of their own poop today." Wolf sipped from her drink. "What's the worst thing you've seen so far?"

"Degloved dick."

"Ew."

The image flashed behind her eyes. A medical photograph. Maybe it wasn't real; people were very good at effects work these days. Within the image was a whole narrative: a man's whole life from his childhood to the moment it was taken, summed up in the image of his penis, skin ripped from it in ... what, an industrial accident? Maybe he stuck it in a thrashing machine, thinking it might get him off. Maybe it did get him off.

On the street outside, a man was advertising some new crypto coin. Nobody even looked at him.

"Ever read Nick Land?" Wolf asked. She was looking at the crypto man as well.

"Never heard of them," Frankie lied.

"I feel like we're living in his world, sometimes." she said.

Frankie was only half-listening, because Vanya had sent her a new picture. Their legs were up in the air and their asshole, entirely hairless, was puckered like the lips of somebody moving in for a kiss. *God fucking damn it they're so hot. I could do anything to them, couldn't I? Fuck...*

She wrote out a text, "are you free this coming week?" It was all wrong though. This little slut wanted to be told what to do. The caption to this new pic was "I'm desperate to see you again i want you rn already.: Make them wait.

"I'll see you next Friday at the White Rabbit pub," she typed, and sent it before she could second-guess herself. It wouldn't be easy waiting that long. It was as much a test of her own resolve as it was an order for Vanya.

At some point between them fucking back at her flat and them both falling asleep, Frankie had asked Vanya how old they were, and they had told her they weren't sure if she was going to like the answer. Her blood had chilled for a moment before Vanya realised how that sounded. No, no, they weren't underage. They were eighteen, nineteen next month.

She tried to imagine what their cock would look like. Their cute little teenage cock. Them begging her not to keep the baby, it would ruin their life, see, they couldn't afford to be a dad. How they'd look when they were pleading for her to abort their kid. The curl of their lip. Razor marks on their arms, maybe. And she'd be like no, I'm keeping it, you're not leaving me, I'm ruining your life. The fantasy expanded out forever, became less about the fetish and instead became something else. The dream of a life. Fucked up.

6

THE RISE AND FALL OF THE TRANS-SEXUAL EMPIRE

There were people out there, in the tumultuous, unending void known as Online, who thought that the bombing attack on the GIC was "fake". How many people? Hard to say. Sometimes it seemed like hundreds, sometimes it seemed to be only a dozen. They all typed in similar ways, and they all seemed to share the same reference points. She wondered if a dozen was an overestimate. Perhaps there was just one loner poster, floating in the nothingness. But then there was so much observable infighting! Everyone seemed to have beef with each other, and it was impossible to track. If it really was only one person, then they were a Grade-A weirdo in Frankie's mind. She spent enough time reading the things they said about her after she got out of hospital that she frequently had nightmares that the bombing genuinely hadn't happened.

They didn't just believe that the bomb was fake. That wasn't enough. A conspiracy is about the story around the event, and so lore was constructed. Frequently it contradicted itself, and this was why most of the community infighting happened. Some of them thought she wasn't a real trans woman. Some believed that the bomb was faked to stoke hate against gender-critical women, or to promote sympathy for trans-identified individuals. Candidates put forward as culprits for the scam included Stonewall and George Soros, though one person claimed, incomprehensibly, that David Attenborough was responsible. Well-meaning people who found her Twitter would send her these posts constantly. *Saw this abt you absolutely disgusting, omg have you seen this absolutely ridiculous Tweet, god I hope ur ok have you looked at what they're saying over there...*

After a while she sent out a tweet asking people to please, *please* stop sending her stuff like that, please stop sending her that *fucking Guardian* article as well, just assume she's seen whatever you want to send her and know that she's been in contact with a legal professional for advice. She hadn't, but that didn't matter, because people were scared off by that. However, she realised, too late, that she missed receiving them. Seeing something so horrific every now and then was good for her soul. She ended up looking the posts up on her own, cutting out the middleman. In one of them, somebody claimed with absolute certainty that Frankie herself had been the one to set the bomb. "The whole thing's a false flag," they said. "Trust me."

~

In the immediate aftermath of the explosion, when she was still in hospital recovering, cops came to see her. They must have been picked especially for her, she thought. There were two of them, a policewoman and a policeman. Both trans.

"So, what can you tell us about it all?" asked the woman.

She sat closest to Frankie's bed and carefully placed her hand palm-down on the mattress next to where Frankie lay. A practised gesture. She was very white and had a thin face with thin eyebrows that looked like she spent a significant amount of time on them. It must take hours every month threading them, cleaning them up. She tried to furrow her brow in a look of concern, but her Botox made the expression a little more sinister than it was probably intended to be.

"I really can't remember much," she said. "I don't even really recall what the ... what she looked like." *But her face is sometimes everywhere, sometimes stapled over the faces of the nurses wheeling people past.* She didn't mention that part. She just wished she could remember what the fucking face *was*.

"It was a woman?" asked the policeman.

"I guess. Middle-aged. She looked like anyone. I don't know how to help you. Wasn't there CCTV?"

He shrugged. "Wasn't turned on."

He was stocky, in a gym-bro sort of way. She only clocked him because the texture and the pattern of his facial hair was recognisable to her. She'd fucked a lot of guys with facial hair like that and had assured them that they looked rugged, and she hadn't had to lie really. It was a hot look.

"She was alone. We get parents coming in on their own sometimes."

It was the story Jade had told her. Her own version of it was reconstructed more from that than her own memories. And Jade's story was just the official story that the cops had heard a hundred times.

The policewoman told her she was being very brave. She was hot as well. They both were, though the guy was more her type.

Would her fantasies of insemination bruise his ego? Some trans guys would have gotten all weird about it; others liked it if she treated them like they were cis fuckboys. She didn't find a way to get his number, but two months later, on one of her first nights back out with the girls, she ran into him at Revenge, and he fucked her with his hairy right fist in the back alley – both literally and euphemistically.

"I want you to knock me up," she had told him then.

"If only I could." he said.

~

When she was seventeen, she'd fucked a Tory MP. She'd fucked a lot of bad men, so fucking some trans guy cop was nothing compared to some of them. Perhaps her personal favourite was a man named Brian Klunsky. That was a juicy memory. She savoured it. It made her cry.

She met Brian in the basement of a flat in Hove. He thought she was a poet, and she didn't correct him. If she had the opportunity, she would have lied to him about being trans, but he must have overheard her talking to someone else. At the time she was gutted about that, but it made the memory so much better. Somehow, they got to talking about modernism. Frankie knew enough to be able to bullshit knowing more, and she was doing a good job by her estimation.

"But Pound was a fascist," she said, sniffing. "Does that not, like ... affect your opinion of him?"

"I agree with you wholeheartedly," said Brian. "But sometimes you have to take the part with the whole. Did you know Poe married his niece? He did, he did. But who can say they aren't chilled and compelled by 'The Masque of the Red Death'."

She shrugged.

"Hmm, maybe not that one. What about 'The Conqueror Worm'? What a poem."

He had a scarf wrapped around his neck, despite how hot it was in the house. She leaned against the wall and next to her was an absurdly tall cheese plant. The air was thick with fag and weed smoke, which couldn't be good for the poor plant. It would go all yellow and shrivel up. She remembered looking at this while he talked about the relative merits of Poe and Pound and how they stacked up against their more *problematic* elements. And then her attention was pulled right back.

"It may seem silly to compare a genius like Pound to a children's author like Jennifer Caldwell, but they both believed in something, and that is one of the things one can't say about half of today's artists."

"What?" Her head was spinning a little. "God, I hate her."

"That doesn't surprise me."

She sniffed. "She's a fucking TERF," she said.

"Ah, there's that word," he said. "All she's doing is asking reasonable questions."

She rolled her eyes. "I was meant to be part of this ... speech festival thing last year," she said. "And one of those TERFS tried to get me fucking banned from it. Caroline Klunsky. I lost out on a load of money ... the speaker's fee."

The man laughed. "Ah, I see. Oh, Caroline ..."

She didn't understand, so he clarified for her. "That's my sister."

"What?"

She thought she could have misheard him; the noise of other people's conversations was encroaching on theirs.

"She is, she is. She's my sister," he chuckled. "I'm Brian Klunsky."

"Fuck."

"Look, I know you think she's evil, but I promise you, she's really alright. Maybe a little bit over-passionate, sometimes, but she is an academic."

"Your *sister*?"

She felt a pain poke into the front of her head for a moment and had to shut her eyes to try and dull it.

"Look," he said, trying to change the subject. "This place is loud. Would you like to talk somewhere quieter?"

"Like where? The garden?" The pain subsided.

"No ..." He looked sheepish. "I meant my room, upstairs."

She didn't even know this was his house. Some part of her knew she shouldn't do this. But as he stood up, so did she, swaying slightly, and she followed him all the way up to his room, a cosy little space with the vibe of a library. The walls were lined with books.

"Do you mind lighting some candles?" he asked her. She did as she was told.

"Do you like trans girls?" she asked while she methodically lit every candle in the room, unsure how many *some candles* meant.

"Oh, I don't know about that. I don't think I've ever, erm ... with one before."

That was clearly not true. But still. She was here now, in his room, with its heavy fabrics and academic texts, and she was on his lap, facing him. He kissed her, and his beard was softer than she expected. His hand slipped up her dress, and she could have sworn he looked pleased when he found her penis there.

He grinned. "Weren't we just talking about Poe? 'A blood-red thing that writhes from out the scenic solitude! It writhes! – it writhes! – with mortal pangs the mimes become its food, and seraphs sob at vermin fangs in human gore imbued.'"

"Sure," she said. *Just get on with it and stop quoting verse at me.* This was back when she had a dick, although the hormones had certainly had their way with it. It wasn't the big, thick rod she'd once owned. It was a small, soft thing. He took off her dress and her panties.

When he kissed her dick, he spoke, very quietly. "That the play is the tragedy, 'Man,' and its hero, the Conqueror Worm."

Shut up about my fucking conquering worm, dude, she thought. It was creepy, but his touch was tender, which she hadn't expected. Then he took her from behind with his hands in her hair. As he did so, she looked straight forward, and saw a row of books on a shelf marked "Gender". *Whipping Girl* and *Gender Trouble*, yes, but side by side with *The Female Eunuch* and the book his sister had just published, about the dangers of erasing "female" as a category. It was enough to make a conspiracist of her – perhaps this was all one big game that everybody around her was playing. A game for only them.

"Daddy?"

He bent over her while he thrust into her gently. "Yes?"

"Will you ... will you get me pregnant?"

To his credit, he took it in his stride. "I don't think you have a choice in the matter." He started to thrust harder.

"I'm your girl, Daddy."

"Yes, yes you are."

"Am I your girl?"

"Yes, you are, you're Daddy's little girlie."

"Am I your fertile little girl?" Tears in her eyes when he said she was.

With each thrust from him, she thought to herself, *I am a traitor, I am a traitor, I am a traitor to the cause.*

7

POSSESSION

There are a few gay pubs in Brighton. Frankie was banned
from one of them, and all the others catered to a clientele
that was decidedly not Vanya's vibe. Older guys, mostly.
Sometimes drag queens, but not the fashionable sort.
There used to be so many more, including lesbian bars and
even a trans bar, but they were long gone. Now it was only
karaoke places and sanitised bullshit bars that looked like
airport lounges. The one she was banned from was the only
half-decent gay pub, and all she'd done was take drugs in
the bathroom. Unfair, in her opinion. As if the staff didn't
get high on shift. That was why she'd said to meet at The
White Rabbit. It was the most aggressively normal pub in
the world. She didn't have to worry that the vibes wouldn't
be right, because there were no vibes at all. It was a neutral
space.

Lula and Jade kept asking about them. They had both seen Vanya on the night, apparently. They'd both seen them leave together. She'd been angry at them, but she couldn't remember what for. When they asked for details, she didn't tell them more than she had to, feigning ignorance of much beyond their name. She realised when she was halfway to the pub that she didn't even know Vanya's surname. It was the first thing she asked when she got there: Niedzwiecki. Vanya Niedzwiecki.

They were waiting for her at a table in the back garden. They didn't have a drink yet. Bless their heart.

Seeing them again, Frankie felt the same as she had that night in the club. The work week had dulled her need a little, but now it rushed back again. The way they looked at her as she walked into the garden, the little shift of excitement. So precious, so perfect. God, if she could put them in a glass box then she would. Maybe in a little cage under her bed. If anyone would say yes to that, it would be Vanya Niedzwiecki.

"Beautiful name," she said. She said it aloud. It felt good on her tongue. "How was your day?"

"So boring," they said. "I just did some gardening for my landlord."

"Oh?"

"He's a friend, really. But he owns the house I live in, and he doesn't charge me rent. In return I do, like, gardening and chores for him."

She wasn't sure if that meant what she thought it meant; it didn't seem like something she could get away with grilling them on now. She filed it away for later and tried her best to crush the jealousy. Vanya wanted a rum and coke, and she got the same. When she came back from the bar with one drink in each hand, she saw them sitting there at the table, looking down at their phone and smoking a cigarette.

"Did I tell you that you could smoke?"

They made the cutest face as they rushed to stub the fag out. She put out her hand and stopped them. Their wrist was so small, she could make a fist around it.

"I'm sorry..." They looked down at the floor, ashamed. They were overplaying it, just a little, but she didn't care.

"I'll let you have one this time," she said. "Roll me one as well. Go on, be a good boy."

The sun was setting behind the row of houses and the sky was full of angry gulls. Vanya was so perfect there, set against the pink and orange of the clouds.

She knew she should tell Jade and Lula everything. Come clean. They were so young, there was such a gulf of experience between them. Both of the girls fucked guys much older than them, so it should be fine to just tell them. They'd be upset if they found out elsewhere ... but they wouldn't find out elsewhere. There'd be no reason to tell them. She didn't have to tell anybody anything about Vanya. She could keep them to herself, keep them private. Other people would have opinions. They'd try to tell her this was all a bad idea. Well, fuck that. Those cunts weren't getting anything. Fuck their support, fuck their solidarity. It only ever came across as patronising.

8

BASH BACK [AN ASIDE]

There were always queers here, but it used to be different. When many places weren't safe for gays, this city was known as a haven. They would flock here when kicked out of their homes, often with no money. Many would work the streets and sleep in communal housing, or wrapped up in blankets out in the frozen sea air. Others would come here to go to university. Others moved here with cash behind them. These ones, the ones in possession of capital, set up businesses, bars, book shops, pubs ... None of them officially gay bars, but all aiming to be genuine sanctuaries. The cops here were less likely to carry out raids on businesses than cops in other parts of the country. The cops here focused on the street sex workers. The gays they arrested were the boys without money, shivering. The boys were terrified, but sometimes grateful for the warmth provided by the cells at least. A complicated gratefulness. The kind of gratefulness that one subjected to violence may have towards a different source of violence.

The gay quarter grew. The bars became teeming centres of nightlife. Cops would walk down the streets, peering at the degenerates they saw, but would not make arrests on the main streets, would not harass the patrons of the bars, at least. The same could not be said for the men. The men would come down from the other side of town, with cricket bats in hand, wearing black shirts, their hair slicked down and shiny, snide grins on their snide faces. And the cops would vanish when they arrived. The men would pace up and down the streets. Sometimes, one of them would feel brave. He would walk up to the windows of a bar known to be a haven for fags, and he would scream, shout, growl, and swing his cricket bat at the glass, shattering it. "This is what you get, you degenerate poofs! First your windows, then your fucking skulls!"

And sometimes it would be skulls. Sometimes some poor sex worker out on the streets would be there, and the men would see him, and he would run, but the men would use the side streets, loop around him, surround him, encroaching in, a circle of black shirts with white faces grinning under moustaches swinging their weapons through the air and do you think the cops ever cared, that in the morning there was another dead pansy on the pavement, blood frozen by the chill, by the morning frost? Another one off the streets.

One day, the gays had enough. They left their houses and their bars. They grouped together, knitting themselves tightly, tightly, tighter than you could believe into one mass, an overwhelming sea. And they walked. They did not wait for the blackshirts to make the journey to them. The throng walked across the town, limbs interlinked, and they got to the gentlemen's club, where they knew the blackshirts met. They kicked at its windows, and at the door, until it splintered. The cops arrived, but they gays were impenetrable, having melded together into one mass of queer flesh, which now grabbed and clawed its way through the fascist house, overturning tables, kicking in the stomachs of Nazi men until they coughed up blood. They pulled logs from the roaring fire, until the carpets caught and went up. They left, and pushed the police away, because the police could not arrest a mass, there was nothing to arrest, no individuals. They were powerless. And as the gay flesh left, the building began to burn with the fascists still inside, many with broken legs, laying on the floors, fire creeping towards them, the heat charring their faces, making their eyeballs run like uncooked eggs. The fire brigade came, but by the time the flames were put out, no one in the building was left alive.

The cops, after that, started to raid the gay bars. But every time they tried, the gays inside would do the same. Cease individuality, just for the time they needed to. Limbs interlocking until the skin was pressed close enough together that it became the same skin. Faces locked in kisses until they became one face. The cops would try to pull at this mass, but to no avail.

This is what we have lost. We have forgotten how to do this, that we even have the power to do it. When homosexuality was legalised, many decided they no longer needed to, and the memory became just that, a memory. Then not even a memory. A story. A vague idea. A metaphor.

9

BEACH

After they left the pub, they walked hand-in-hand to the beach. It was dark now. There was a tiny glow illuminating the sky at the furthermost stretch of the horizon, but even that was nearly gone. The gulls were screaming like murder victims, sometimes swooping down so low that she thought one might carry Vanya away from her. They were both drunk, so the walk took longer than it should have. Vanya clung to her side. Their phone kept buzzing.

They sat together on the pebbles, looking out to sea. The further out it went, the rougher it got.

"Can I ask you something?"

Frankie stroked their hair. "Sure."

"Have you ever had a parasite?"

"Weird question."

"Yeah … You don't have to answer if you don't want to."

They bit their lip.

"It's fine. I guess I had nits and worms as a kid ... I told you what I do for a living, right? Well, I saw something gross the other day. Something parasitic. I don't even know if it was real. But it was a video of some sort of worm being pulled out of a guy's urethra."

Vanya's nails dug into the palm of her hand.

"Really? Can you remember anything else about it?"

"Not really, sorry. I try not to pay too much attention. I see some pretty gnarly stuff on a day- -to-day basis."

The wind rolled in around them, and a group of people further up the beach, nearer the pier, were howling like wolves.

"Come on," she said. "I want to fuck you again."

"H-here?"

She grabbed their face. "Don't question me, okay? I get what I want. There's a good boy."

They kissed, but the buzzing of their phone cut through the moment. Frankie pushed them back, away from her. Not violently and not very far, but enough to show that she was unhappy.

"Turn your fucking phone off."

"I ... I can just set it to silent."

"No," she said, firmly. "Turn it off, now."

"But—"

"Turn it off immediately, Vanya Niedzwiecki. I won't ask again." They looked like they might cry. Bless their heart. But they did what they were told. Whoever was blowing up their phone – their landlord probably – would have to wait their fucking turn. This time, the kissing was perfect. Everything was as it was meant to be.

10

CURIOUS CAT

ANON asked @Grillsheep: Have you ever had a parasite?

@Grillsheep answered: No I haven't lol sorry

ANON asked @spiroaddict69: Have you ever had a parasite?

@spiroaddict69 answered: I guess I had worms when I was a kid … is that what you mean? Weird q tbh

ANON asked @recoverbunny: Have you ever had a parasite?

@recoverbunny answered: Yeah I gave myself a tapeworm a few years ago when I had rlly bad anorexia but tbh it didn't stay in there for v long before I shat it out. Was kind of upset at first but I didn't like having it much, felt sick all the time and stuff ... guess that's the weird thing about EDs ... you feel sick all the time and in pain and stuff and your like this is how I should feel this means its working this is right. Sorry kind of a long answer there haha

ANON asked @sunnyspwingle: Have you ever had a parasite?

@sunnyspwingle: I got nits rn

ANON asked @malcolminthexmiddle: Have you ever had a parasite?

@malcolminthexmiddle answered: ???????????? what kinda question is this

ANON asked @queenfan333: Have you ever had a parasite?

@queenfan333 answered: [GIF of a minion blowing a raspberry with its mouth] get raspberried creepy bitch

ANON asked @lpoaaaptera: Have you ever had a parasite?

@lpoaaaptera answered: Well I was pregnant once ... does a fetus count? 😄

ANON asked @mimosars: What would you do if you had rare parasite and doctor said you had to live witbh it so they could study it?

@mimosars answered: Wut

ANON asked @whiteteethbyzadiesmith: What would you do if you had rare parasite and doctor said you had to live witbh it so they could study it?

@whiteteethbyzadiesmith answered: Ummm are they gonna pay me to live with it because if they paid me a lot of money yeah. Guess it would be like being a surrogate .... creepy idea though. You should write a horror film about it!

ANON asked @daddyslilblorbo: What would you do if you had rare parasite and doctor said you had to live witbh it so they could study it?

@daddyslilblorbo answered: Sounds kinda HOT imo!

ANON asked @chewchewchrain: What would you do if you had rare parasite and doctor said you had to live witbh it so they could study it?

@chewchewchrain answered: Is this a fetish thing?? Stop fetish mining weirdo. Also youre fetish is FUCKIN CREEPY

ANON asked @bigdicksal: What would you do if you had rare parasite and doctor said you had to live witbh it so they could study it?

@bigdicksal answered: Wouldn't live with it obvs I don't want some weird fuckin parasite that's why I divorced my husband

ANON asked @911real: IM WORRIED I HAVE RINGWORM HELP

@911real answered: What do you want me to do about it lol just go to the doctor

ANON asked @gibbotruther: IF you had a tapeworm inside of your body and you were gonbna get rid of it but tghen suddenly it started to talk to you nand you realised it was SENTIENT would you still gety rid of it?

@gibbotruther answered: You sent me this message ten fucking times anon. I saw it. im not going to answer it. give up

ANON asked @911real: I'M WORRIED I MIGHT HAVE INSECT EGGS UNDER MY SKIN HELP

@911real answered: Not this again .....

ANON asked @gayfrogaftermath: in my house my children appreciate their lice and their worms for what tbhey are: a gift. When they7 first got them I decided to teach them how important it was to be kind and giving to others ... and that having these things could be so good ... when I got co mplauints from their schpol that otbher students seemed ti be catching things from them I knew what I was doing was right ... mty daughter when she first grew puboc hair I put pubic lice on her and she said MUMMy they feel so funny they tickle and she giggled and I dsaid that's good now do youy know what to do and she said yes mummy I have to pass trhem on ...

@gayfrogaftermath answered: I've looked up your IP address, if youre telling the truth then the police will be coming to take your kids away because it sounds like you shouldn't have kids what the hell!!! Ive reported you

ANON asked @911real: THEYRE INSIDE ME THEYRE HATCHING

@911real answered: Fuck off omg

ANON asked @911real: IT FEELS SOO WEIRD ... THEYRE ALL CRAWLING ABOUT UIN MY ... 981 CAN SEE TRHEM UNDER MY SKIN

@911real answered: ...

ANON asked @recoverbunny: whatr you said about having had a tapewoirm whem you had anorwxia I relate to that so much I did the same except I kept it and I loved that it wa\s inside me it Mad3e my pussy sooo wet it made me so wet and my girlfrue nds who also had anoexia also she got one too and her pussy was so wet by the whole thing NSD WER userd to trib all day long yuntil she broke UP with me the BITCH THWE BITCH THE B8ITCH

@recoverbunny answered: It ... sounds like you are a man pretending tro be a girl. Please get off my page this is a page for advice about recovering from eating disorders/

ANON asked @recoverbunny: umm men can have eating disorders too don't be so bigoted

@recoverbunny answered: I know but he was pretending to be a girl talking abt getting off on having a tapeqworm lol im not saying men cant have eds

ANON asked @recoverbunny: it sounded like that's what you were saying is all no need to get so defencive

@recoverbunny answered: If you people keep up im goinna have to turn off anonymous questions jesus

ANON asked @redflagworldover: CONFESSION TIME .... I have a kink for having parasites and giving other people parasites ... I love it so much I love the thought of it I cant get enough of it .. is that normal?

@redflagworldover answered: Nothings normal bitch idk. Man fascism is on the rise and youre out here worrying about some kink you have? Who cares. Just do it with other people who like it and shuit up I don't wanna be a part of this.

11

CARRION COMFORT

This isn't normal. It wasn't. She didn't feel like this about people. But Vanya wasn't a normal person. If she hadn't met them in a public place she might wonder if they were a ghost or a hallucination. Jade and Lula had seen them, though, so they must be real. The girls kept quizzing her in the group chat.

"Weee saw you leave with them and they looked pretty young eyes emoji"

They're twenty-one, Frankie replied. That was all they were getting.

Pretty young for u, typed Lula. *& a 2nd date???? who are you and what have you done with Francesca Dunwich lol.*

A week from that first date and they met again. Frankie liked the idea of spacing things out a week apart. It felt like pacing herself. It did mean that the work week was somehow even more gruelling than ever before. The cold concrete walls of her office didn't do anything to help. If they bothered to paint them at least, or infuse the room with some life or colour, maybe it would be easier to cope with. She'd worked a lot of bullshit jobs, but this one stuck out for the sheer lack of effort put into all the bullshit.

Each day turned into the next. A transphobic thread was reported to her, and she read the whole thing five times over just because of how confusing it was:

... the swing of a butcher's knife. From "top surgery" to tweets about abortions for likes. It is not enough to have everything. It must dream about what it cannot. They find joy in denigrating the bodies that grew them and burrow into dreams of abortions with the joy of a blowfly in cadaverous ecstasy. This thing that speaks like carrion dreaming of dead flesh. This dream that sounds like the raw rasp or tearing sinews, the wet yawn or ripped muscle, the discordant busy buzz of a fly transformed made mad by the scent of the dead.

It was written so strangely that it impressed her. It was better than most of the shit guys like that tended to churn out. They usually just repeated the same points and phrases. This guy, well, he was original, and the imagery stayed with her. She kept having fantasies of touching her own cunt and finding it slick and wet. But she couldn't get wet, she knew that in the fantasy. Her fingers would come away and she would see that they were covered in blood. She would feel the pain, suddenly sharp in her abdomen, and know that even after all this time her body had somehow decided, or realised, that her cunt was a cut in between her thighs.

Another fantasy, one that started the same: she would go to touch herself and find that her skin had sealed her pussy shut after her brain had registered it as a wound, and she would press her fingers on the blank fresh clean skin where her genitals should have been. Her urethra would be sealed shut too, and her piss would build up inside of her until her bladder burst, flooding her insides and causing them to go septic. She would have to take a knife and cut the skin away from where it had grown over her lips and her clit, carefully so as not to cut open the vulva itself. If her hand slipped then ... the wet yawn, the ripped muscle. The carrion comfort.

~

Vaccines caused autism. 5G controls women's periods. Racist meme. She was just a robot. Misleading statistic. Picture of a dead dog, beheaded. Blood on the white dust of the road. Cross burned into a woman's cadaver. A lot of people post pictures of injured, dead, or dying people online. She saw so many each week, but only one had ever truly fucked her up – a girl who had made it back on various social media platforms, gotten all sorts of sponsorship deals with all sorts of weight-loss health teas that made you shit out your guts. A boy started commenting on her pictures on Instagram, telling her how beautiful she was. She received many such comments. He tried to message her, but she never saw the messages. They ended up in her endless pile of requests, a place she never looked (correctly, for her own health). The boy kept messaging. Kept commenting. But what you have to understand is that his behaviour was not unusual; it was what many people did to her, for many different reasons, and she had learned by this point to only briefly look at what people said about her. Sometimes a friend would message her asking if she knew there was now a whole subreddit dedicated to posting pictures of her and analysing them, and speculating about her sex life and her whereabouts, and she would say that she knew but she preferred not to hear about it.

Here is what happened next: that one boy, one of many, one of countless, posted on the subreddit that he had matched with her on Tinder. There were incredulous, disbelieving comments. *No way dude your way too mid* and *she doesn't use tinder lol you fell for a catfish*. The boy posted a picture of the profile. The comments were still sceptical. He posted a screenshot of their conversation. No one believed that it was her – partly, of course, because they hated the idea that one of their own could actually talk to her, something which had always seemed completely out of the realm of possibility. If he really had matched with her, that would have broken the bonds of their subreddit. It should have been rule number one. No one ever actually talks to her. She is not sexually available to us. The idea that one of their number had crossed this boundary spiralled them into self-hate. "Why him and not us?" they asked. The last screenshot he posted was of her agreeing to meet up with him. She didn't realise that he was a fan of hers. She thought he didn't know who she was at all. Then: silence.

Someone joked that he would wake up the next day naked in an abandoned warehouse minus a few organs. The next day he posted an image of the girl lying in the back of a car, wearing a little black dress, a deep wound across her neck which had nearly but not completely severed her head from her body. The image had the caption "got her". It was quickly deleted, but soon afterwards it was reposted by more users, speculating on its potential realness. It was posted elsewhere too. That was how she had seen it. It had been reported and it came to her to look at. When she had seen the image, it had been used to illustrate a user's point that the lifestyle of influencers was dangerous and led only to misery and death.

Got her.

~

This time, Vanya came over to her flat, which was a fairly small one bed near St Peter's Church. Her flat was a mess when she got back from work, and she was just about to start cleaning up ready for Vanya to arrive when she realised she didn't need to. It didn't fucking matter at all. She could just tell them to do it, and they would.

Later, they lay on her bed together. She had lit some incense in the room, so everything smelled like a shop that sold crystals. It was nice.

"God, look at you," Frankie said, stroking their hair. "You're my little doll." Someone had said similar to Frankie once – a thirty-three-year-old gay man who took her in early in her transition, when she had just run away from home. She felt like she really was his little doll, made of porcelain and slightly cracked. He was very careful with her; he kept her safe. Or he tried to. He was dead now.

"I am?"

"Dolls don't talk. Stay still now."

Frankie brushed their hair, slowly. Vanya tried their best to breathe shallow breaths, because dolls did not breathe. It was sweet that they didn't even need to be told to do that, that they just did it instinctively.

Frankie continued talking. "I never got to play with dolls as a little girl. I wasn't allowed to play with them. But now I do get to play with dolls. I get to play with you."

She noticed that she hadn't heard their phone buzz. Good. She hoped it was turned off instead of being on silent, but they hadn't checked it in front of her. Lesson learned, then.

She put lipstick on their mouth. Not cleanly, not well. It was a red smear. Frankie had never been good at putting on makeup, she'd always been a bad trans woman in that way. On very bad days she didn't feel affirmed at all by makeup: she felt like a clown, a dancing clown. But she wasn't trying to do a good job here, she was *playing*, in the same way a child plays with makeup. Vanya stayed as still as they could, and afterwards, when Frankie let them break character, they gasped before demanding a mirror.

"You made me look wild," they laughed, looking at themself. "I don't hate it, though. It's avant-garde."

"Do I hear a hint of sarcasm?"

"No, I'd never be a brat like that," they said. "I promise."

Silverfish scurried across her ceiling above them while they fucked. The windows were smeared with water stains from old condensation. The room smelled damp, but the sweaty smell of sex began to change that. Her curtains were still open. Outside, the moon was clear but there were no stars. None at all.

"You're my fucking *whore*," Frankie said, as she thrust the dildo into Vanya's arsehole.

"I – I'm your fucking whore? Am I?"

"You're my fucking whore."

They were crying. Their face was puffy and red, and spit was dribbling out of their open mouth.

"Please," they said. "Mummy please."

She grabbed them by the hair with their free hand, but she went too hard and their face was slammed right into the wall. *Fuck*. They flopped onto the bed, head upturned but not moving. Blood was oozing from their nose. Their eyes seemed glassy.

"Vanya?" They looked like a corpse. They were so still, and so perfect. She could have kept fucking them ... Not that she would do that, but she could have.

"What?"

"Are you okay? You hit your head," she said.

"It's fine." They pulled themselves up and wiped the blood from their face. "Oh ... I'm bleeding. Do you like that?"

"I ..."

More blood kept coming out of their nose. "What?"

"I'm sorry," said Frankie.

"Why?"

"Because I hurt you."

"I don't care." They were looking out of the window. "It's fine, really. It's what God made me for."

When they started kissing again, Frankie went on top of them. Vanya's body was so white and cold, and the blood was drying on their skin. Frankie would have felt like a necrophile if it hadn't been for the slight smile that showed at the corner of their lips when they looked up at her. That's how she knew they were alive.

12

A UNIQUE CASE
OF BRITISH DISEASE

It was late enough that the moths were out. She saw them on the little walk between the tube station and her destination. There seemed to be more in the side streets, the areas where the busy traffic and loud students melted away and were replaced by a sort of suburban silence. Big moths, too, some of them. Big and dark. As she walked under one streetlight, which must have only flickered on a short while ago, she saw one of the moths zoom suddenly fast right into the bulb. It bounced off but she heard it *thump*. Perhaps there were bats here too, or perhaps the reason for the moths' population boom was precisely that there weren't any natural predators here. Samantha was a predator. An unnatural one. In the windows of one of the parked cars she passed, her head was tiny, and her torso and legs were huge like a gigantic cone.

A funhouse mirror vision of what a woman might look like, which was something Arthur had called her once, when he had been sozzled and could barely look her in the eye.

Halfway down the road was a wide gap between houses. In the gap was a gate, and through the gate were more houses. The mortgage on any house here must be extortionate, but the ones in the little gated mews probably constituted more money than she'd ever had in her fairly comfortable middle-class life. She rang the buzzer on the gate and said her name into the little intercom, and then the gate swung open automatically. Its hinges sounded like they needed some WD-40 or something because they creaked all the while, like the doors to a haunted house in a campy old film. She saw the porch light go on above the front door of one of the houses in the mews, the one at the far end of the little cobbled street. Even from here she could see the way the moths flocked to it instantly. The door opened and a figure in shadow stepped out. It raised an arm and swung it either in a wave at Samantha or as an attempt to swat away the moths. She wasn't sure, so she waved back and walked in the figure's direction.

"Oh, hi..." said the woman when she got close enough for each of them to see the other. "You're *Sam* – right?"

"Samantha," she said. There was an awkward little beat of nothing. "Sam's fine, though."

"Good," said the woman, with a little wry smile. "Come inside! Everybody else is already here."

Samantha followed her into the house. One of the moths had made it in and was now desperately throwing itself against the light in the hallway. It was pathetic and sad. If it had been her house, she would have gently ushered it out, but the woman didn't even acknowledge it. Samantha told her that her house was lovely, and the woman thanked her.

When Samantha spoke, it was in a voice very carefully crafted to sound as meek as possible. Her voice trainer had made her put together a mood board for it. It had been full of old illustrations of church mice, drawings done to go along with nursery rhymes. Her trainer had looked at the images and said she knew exactly what Samantha wanted, and the voice that had been created over the course of the training sounded as close as she could get to those images. It had been pretty much perfect for a little while, but now she was starting to age her voice seemed to be getting deeper despite itself, and so Samantha spoke even quieter, every word pronounced as softly as humanly possible, like she was scared she might startle somebody.

The woman was already at the end of the corridor now and heading down a flight of stairs. For whatever reason, she hadn't offered to take Samantha's coat, so Samantha stopped and hung it herself from one of the golden hooks on the wall to her right. There were lots of coats already there; only one of the hooks wasn't tripled down with them. She hung hers carefully on it, trying to guess which coat belonged to which person, as the woman descended the stairs without looking back to check if Samantha was following. When Samantha did go after her, she walked carefully and softly, trying to avoid what she had heard someone once term the *flat-footed thumping of men's steps.* Ever since that phrase had been uttered in her earshot, it had wormed its way into the front of her head. Every time she was walking in public or around other people, she remembered it and adjusted accordingly.

The stairs were lined with paintings of pastoral scenes, which went, rather elegantly she thought, from day at the top of the stairs to night at the bottom, where the dining room and kitchen were. The dining room opened out into a large garden, or as large as was reasonably attainable for a London townhouse situated on a slope, which was why the garden was a whole level below the front door. A quirk of the borough. The road itself was level, but the road exactly parallel to it was a full storey lower, and so on from there, all the way down to the heath. Marx's head was down there, somewhere. The Marx head no longer had a nose, she knew that. Some guy had attacked it with a hammer, and nobody had bothered to repair it. In fact, there had been murmurings from some corners about removing it all together.

She came to the bottom of the stairs and saw all of them there already, assembled around the table, chatting and drinking. There were only three empty spaces. Everyone looked up as she entered the room and gazed straight at her. Men and women, looking at her.

"Hi Sam," one of them said. Jean. The woman who owned the house, the one who had opened the door for her, was named Lily. She saw these people rarely, and mainly interacted with them on Twitter. She matched their faces to their profile images and the names associated with them. Kenneth.

Helen. Paloma. Scott. A second Helen. Kathy. A third Helen. A Helena. No Jennifer. She wondered if Jennifer wasn't coming after all, but then she heard Lily say, "Jen's just texted saying she'll be a little later." Samantha took her place. The wine bottle was on the table; she had to pour her own glass, it seemed, but at least they'd left one in front of her seat.

She was the only transsexual here, and she knew that some of the people in the room wouldn't even want to call her that, except maybe begrudgingly, because they didn't want to call her a man in drag to her face. They'd happily call other people men in drag to their faces, but not her, because she would join in, and that meant she was invited to things like this, got to sit at their table and drink from their flutes and sometimes write a piece for *The Times*. Once Kenneth, who, at this moment, when she was sitting down at the table, was purposefully looking elsewhere, had put his hand on her hip and said that she was one of the better ones and then made to kiss her before stumbling away into a taxi. She had felt sick later that night, knowing that she wished he'd kept going, but that he was more drunk than her, that no one ever seemed to want to kiss her unless they were that drunk, and even then, they didn't want to follow through.

She drank from her glass. The windows into the garden were open, and as the night was coming down, moths started to flutter in around the strip lighting in the ceiling. Her head hurt looking at the lights for too long. Her head hurt now whenever she opened Twitter, just a twinge, but what of it. She didn't use it because she wanted to.

"I think we're seeing real progress," said Helen 2, "especially now we have so many ministers that agree with us. The big issue is how many agree with us but don't do anything about it, you know. They just agree with us, sometimes like our tweets, and take flack for that. But then when we're out on the streets yelling, where are they to be seen?"

"Well," Helena said, "that's why Jennifer is so good. Not a minister, true, but she might as well be."

"Probably more powerful than a minister."

"Probably."

Everyone nodded in agreement. Samantha did too, but she kept her mouth shut. Every time she spoke without being directly asked a question around these people, she felt their eyes stabbing into her, as if her simply speaking, almost always in agreement, was grossly offensive. She did agree with them! But she supposed sometimes that wasn't good enough. She couldn't hate them for thinking of her as a man because she too thought of herself as a man often enough, and with what was likely to be far more ferocious intensity than any of them could muster. Sometimes, recently, the inside of her skull seemed to be a constant repeating thought that was simply *man man man man* whenever she saw herself in the reflection of, say, a shop window, or a car door, or or or. She could see herself faintly in the glass of her drink. She could hear what Helen 1 was thinking when she looked at her.

"What do you think other right-minded transsexuals like you have to do?" Helen 1 asked, looking right at her.

A moth was fluttering about above the woman's head, a large one, white with black spots across its wings, and in the light it looked larger still than it probably was. Samantha swallowed her mouthful of wine.

"Well," she said, making sure her voice was neither too loud nor too deep, "I do think we are trying. You know, every time I see someone being misogynist in the name of transsexual causes, I tell them what they're doing. I try to distribute as much feminist writing as I can to other transsexuals who perhaps might be potentially persuaded or do not have much of a political engagement. But it's an uphill battle. I think the lines are getting further apart. And what's worse is that I see so many of them, transactivists, transgenderists, now calling themselves transsexuals proudly, some of them without even bothering to go through the process. Which is quite offensive, really."

"But what are you doing to combat the misogyny?"

"I mean, calling it out, as I said. Every time I see it. Do you ... think I, we, could be doing more?"

"Yes," said Helen.

"What?"

"I think that's more on you to answer," she said.

Lily cut in. "We're very grateful to have you," she said. "You're wonderful company and you speak so well on things."

She knew that they used her to prove a point. That was why she was invited to speak at things. It wasn't that they liked her. Lily only cut in now because Helen was speaking too close to the actual fact of things.

If you know they hate you, Samantha, if you know why they always shorten your name to Sam, why come here at all? Why not disengage? Let the transsexual tide turn away from you? Become anonymous? Delete Twitter?

Kenneth sent her a picture of his flaccid penis once, unprompted, asking if she thought that mole was anything to worry about.

"No, you're right," she said. "Helen's right. We do need to do more. But I don't want to get in the way, you know. I don't want to dominate the conversation. I don't want to make anyone uncomfortable, so sometimes I just sit back and let you talk, make sure my presence makes things clear that transsexuals *do* agree with you. But yes. We can do more."

The moth landed on the very top of Helen's head.

"There's a moth in your hair," Samantha said.

Helen's hand shot up and grabbed it in her fist, as fast as anything Samantha had seen. She moved her hand away and tightened it, crushing the moth between her fingers and her palm. It was such a strange, sudden action that Samantha found herself unsure if she was going to say anything more, or if her little speech was finished. Helen opened her hand and let the crushed insect fall onto the table. It was barely recognisable as a moth anymore, just a mass of brown stuff squished into a ball.

"What?" asked Helen.

"Oh, just ... that was fast," smiled Samantha.

"I hope Jen arrives soon," said Scott from the far end of the table, evidently bored of anything she had to say.

Jen. Jennifer Caldwell, valiant high priestess of the movement (such as there was a movement). Samantha had been around her a couple of times now, but she had never spoken a word to her, had only smiled and nodded politely before turning off to speak to someone else. Nevertheless, Samantha had read everything she had ever written, despite not having any interest in children's fantasy literature. It was practically a rule if you wanted to be respected as a Gender Critic. If you were on a video chat and you didn't have Caldwell's books framed clearly behind you, whatever council there was that decided things around here would probably subject you to some form of disciplinary action.

Caldwell had written twelve books about a little girl and her witch friends, which started off mostly whimsical and ended up as strangely violent holocaust allegories in which witches were burned alive in ovens. Samantha found those sickening, in all honesty, but Jennifer was Jennifer after all. Once those books were finished, she continued writing but for adults now, working on a series of books about farming life. Critics either thought these books were shockingly dull or wonderfully witty. Five years ago, Caldwell had, reportedly, contacted Helen 1, who had written an article for *The Telegraph Online* about women's prisons. Caldwell had questions for Helen – the article had made her feel shocked and scared in a way things rarely did. She started to read and converse with the gender-critical side more often, although always in private, until recently, when she had come out publicly through her work. In her latest rural satire, there had been an extended plot thread about a man who dressed as a woman to enter a WI meeting. Once she began facing criticism from TRAs, Caldwell started to be more public about her beliefs around trans women, sex workers, socialists, and anti-Zionist wonks. Helen 2 had painted a picture of Jennifer, haloed by golden light, surrounded by hordes of grateful women bowing their heads. Scott had become quite grumpy about the whole thing, given that, before Jennifer went public with her beliefs, he had been by far the most famous individual in their loose circle of intellects.

The knowledge that Jennifer (Jennifer!) would be here soon had charged the dining room with an electric energy. Everyone was shifting and moving and trying to get comfortable, and the conversations were quiet and brief. See, nobody wanted to say anything important when Jennifer wasn't within earshot. This was what had happened: the group had restructured itself around its new celebrity member, centring her suddenly, and side-lining others. Members of the group felt a mix of emotions about this. Many were resentful that someone so relatively new to the ideology, with more undeveloped thoughts, was now its de-facto leader. Many too were jealous that Caldwell enjoyed the benefits of her wealth, in the billions, while some of them had faced losing their jobs for their beliefs. The finale of the film series of adaptations of her children's fantasy novels was coming out soon. A journalist and opinion writer had said that the film was a torch in the darkness of today's growing fascism, and compared the current prime minister to Rasputin, the books' antagonist.

Jennifer Caldwell walked with ten thousand shining wings fluttering at her back. Jennifer Caldwell rose with her red hair, and ate men like air. They could all feel the pulsing through the earth as Jennifer Caldwell got closer and closer, her taxi turning onto the street. When she passed a streetlight, its light bulged and burst through its proximity to her. She sucked the breath from your lungs. She crushed pimps and traffickers beneath her sensible shoes. She struck through Stonewall and the BDS movement with a sword made of pure and blinding light.

Nobody had anything to say. There was nothing anyone could hope to say. They all awaited Jennifer until they heard the bell ring out, signalling her imminent arrival. Lily disappeared up the stairs, nearly tripping over herself in her rush towards the front door. When she was gone, they all held their breath, and Samantha wished for a strange moment that they might all put out their hands and clasp them together so that they formed an unbroken ring. Lily reappeared, scurrying down the stairs, and behind her came Jennifer like a walking god, a walking Twitter account, a thing with billions upon billions of pounds and clout and influence, a hot, wet, dripping *woman* made from *woman* bits. A normal woman, an adult human female. She was material. You could, if you liked, reach out and touch her, but Samantha wouldn't ever do that. It was hard enough just existing in its presence, this pure and unfiltered ideal of modern womanhood. Normal and extranormal. Reality and the breaking thereof. A Corbynite on Twitter had once called her *a remarkable case of British disease*.

"Hello everyone," she said in that jovial voice of hers. Jennifer looked around the room slowly. Her gaze brushed across each of them in turn. A blessing. When she looked at each person, she nodded at them. Kenneth let out a little yelp when she did that at him, which Samantha thought was pathetic, but nobody commented on it. And then her gaze fell upon Samantha, and not only did she nod but she spoke to her, said her name. "Hello, Samantha," she said. Her full name! No shortened, ambiguously gendered *Sam* here, but *Samantha*.

"Hi," she said, in a quiet voice.

"It's so good to see you," Jennifer said.

"It's good to see you too."

"I'm glad to see you didn't start without me," she said to the room.

"We wouldn't dream of it," said the Helens as one, their voices aligned perfectly in pitch and tone and rhythm.

"He doesn't know a thing, does he?" Jennifer looked at Samantha sharply when she spoke those words.

"Nope," said Kenneth. "You know once we were drunk after an event, and he tried to pull me into a taxi with him? He had his hands around my waist and everything."

"I just hate when he speaks, you know," said Lily. "He always speaks so loudly, and so deeply, a loud, deep voice, speaking over everyone else."

They were moving in on her now. Samantha looked around and saw the three Helens hop up on top of the table, crouched, arms towards her, creeping forwards. Kenneth and Scott were either side of her. All of them, encircling her, while Jennifer looked on from above like the eye of God gazing down.

"I don't understand!" shouted Samantha, looking for somewhere to run to, but there was nowhere to go. They were creeping up on her from every side. Their hands were nearly touching her.

"You're a man, Sam," said Lily.

"S-so's Kenneth! So's Scott!"

Lily spat at her. It hit her in the cheek. It was so warm. "But at least they admit it," she said.

Samantha wiped the spit away and looked behind her, but there was nothing. Nothing at all to grab, nowhere to run to. No hope. And then they were upon her.

Samantha fell to the floor, scrabbling and pushing against them, but to no avail. They were pressing down on her firmly. Both men had her arms, and the Helens were sitting on her legs. She was looking up into their faces and she recognised something there that she hadn't recognised before. There were ... *things* visible in their eyes. There were *things* dripping out of their mouths. In their pockets and bags their phones throbbed with notifications, messages and BREAKING NEWS alerts saying that two men, a couple, had been found dead in a park in Islington. A strange clear liquid dribbled down all their cheeks as they looked at their respective screens for a moment before turning their attentions back to her. Jennifer bent down so that she was closer to Samantha than either of them wanted her to be.

"Don't listen to them. Just let them air their silly frustrations. It's not because of anything you've done. There's nothing you can atone for. In fact, I like you, Sam. So, I'll tell you this: I've been privy to something. And I can tell you, it's going to get *worse*."

She grinned. The things were in her mouth too, and she dribbled that horrible liquid. "So, so much worse. We've decided that, given you're *one of the good ones*, we'd spare you the horrors to come."

One of the things dripped from her open mouth and landed right in Samantha's eye. It squirmed there, agitated and confused. It was a worm.

"Oh, let me get that for you." Jennifer picked it right out of her eye and popped it back into her mouth. "Anyway. Don't worry. It's nothing personal."

Can you feel it coming?

In the earth?

Through the sky?

Boiling in the rising ocean?

I heard someone tell it to me a while ago, and I didn't believe them because it couldn't be true. Surely this is just the way things are, they have always been like this, and this is the way things always will be. Naive, stupid, childish way of thinking.

But now I know it like doctrine, I know it to be true and they all do as well, even if they enjoy the sad spectacle in the moment.

This fucking country, man.

This fucking world.

In the earth, air, sea, on the forums and the local council Facebook groups, one truth becomes clear, one truth above everything else, and once you know it you cannot un-know it: it's getting worse.

The women and the few men all hooked their fingers, gnashed their teeth like rabid beasts. They pulled out knives from hidden places.

It's getting worse.

They pounced and began to tear into Samantha. She screamed but nobody cared to hear. Just another dead degenerate. Not the first and not the last. Not the last, not by a long shot.

After it was done, Jennifer and Lily and Kenneth and all the others couldn't help it. They were far too excited to go back to sitting and drinking wine. When they kissed, the worms reached between their eyes and mouths like threads that connected them, binding them together in this fucked-up dream. Samantha's body hadn't even entered rigor mortis when they started to fuck.

PART TWO

GUTWORMS

In an introduction to *Studies on Hysteria* written in 1893, Freud identifies the repressed itself as a foreign body. Noting that hysterical symptoms replay some original trauma in response to an accident, Freud explains that the memory of trauma 'acts like a foreign body which, long after its entry, must continue to be regarded as an agent that is still at work.' In other words, until an original site of trauma reveals itself in therapy, it remains foreign to body and mind but active in both. The repressed, then, figures as a sexual secret that the body keeps from itself and it figures as foreign because what disturbs the body goes unrecognized by the mind.

Jack Halberstam, *Skin Shows: Gothic Horror and the Technology of Monsters*

"The living wash in vain, in vain perfume themselves, they stink."

Samuel Beckett, 'First Love'

1

LESBIAN MASTERDOC

He told you that you were born fucked in the head & you believed
him. It sounded true. You took him at his word. He told you then
that you were born with a dick in your brain & it was a few years
later before you realised he was quoting a fucking Eminem song
at you & you felt like such an idiot. But hey you thought he was
still right in a way it wasn't wrong you were born with a dick
in your brain. You were born fucked in the head. So what. Was
there from the very start from the moment you were dragged
from her cunt into the disappointing light of the maternity ward
& even then it was already hard but it got worse as time went on.
In your early teens your sex began to hurt you. You have since
heard people compare the sexual awakening of a young girl to
the poetic image of a flower opening in springtime but you aren't
a girl & even if you were your experience was so far removed from

that it's fucking laughable. You've never been a flower. You weren't connected to the moon. It oozed out of you. Your cycle was not a source of power it was like a monthly fucking miscarriage.

You used to stare at girls. You started doing that when you were very young. You used to stare at them until they noticed & felt uncomfortable & you kind of liked that you made them feel uncomfortable. If she noticed she would tell you to stop, sometimes you did, usually you couldn't you didn't have a choice in the matter. You can remember one day you were in the city centre running errands with her & a woman walked past & you saw her tits through her thin vest you saw her hard visible nipples you saw her ass jiggle as she walked you saw her avoid the man trying to get her to sign up for donations to Macmillan Cancer Support you saw her you watched her as Mum had a fag you watched her walk past you her hair was black it did not reflect the sun. Then she saw you looking and sucking on the lollipop you had in your mouth you can even remember the flavour it was strawberry in your memory. You saw her see you looking. The journey of her face. Why is she looking at me? Why is she staring? Then she was gone. Mum asked you what you were doing. I was just looking at her ... It's rude to stare! *No it isn't.* Girls ... don't stare at girls like that. *Then* I'm not a girl *was what you thought. It probably wasn't but once you know more about yourself you think back on this incident & you insert that thought into it which makes it easier. Instead you just stood there gormless mindless freak sucking on your strawberry lollipop until Mum filled with such rage at Her burgeoning little dyke of a daughter grabbed the sweet right out of your mouth & threw it into the closest City*

Council Bin MUMMY! *you screamed too late not that She'd have changed her mind anyway not that She could have changed the track Her actions were on you were horrified you wished you'd bit Her fingers you ran towards the bin and looked down into it at your lollipop it glimmered down there it was still wet from your spit but going sticky the bin smelled rancid you weren't thinking you reached out your hand down into the dark to get your sweetie back but Mum pulled you away horrified that people must have noticed what just happened Mum scolding saying Vanya! Vanya! What are we going to do with you? Oh Christ. Disgusting child. Disgusting. You took those words to heart.*

2

BLOODSUCKING FREAK

The woods past Stanmer House were beautiful. They marked the beginning of the South Downs, the great, low, rolling hills that cover that corner of the country. Stanmer village itself was nestled in a valley. It was, to be honest, quite a lifeless little place, devoid of much to see or do beyond the small churchyard that boasted two yew trees, and a shit café. There wasn't even a pub. It may as well have been the set of a television show, with the people who lived there just actors tasked with *playing* the inhabitants of a typical quaint English village. When Frankie and Vanya walked down Stanmer's main road, that was all she could think about on seeing the locals sitting in their front gardens or walking their dogs. *You aren't real people, these are not the lives of real people.* But Vanya hadn't asked to walk out here to see the village. It was the Downs they had begged to see.

It was pretty stunning, Frankie had to admit. She had lived close by for ages but could never be arsed to drag herself here. It was just a short bus ride away, though, and all the traffic and the air pollution disappeared. She had been surprised Vanya wanted to come out there so badly. But now that both of them were there, Frankie was glad she'd gone along with it. Vanya looked gorgeous, framed against the green. They skipped through the tall, dry grass, disturbing grasshoppers as they went.

~

The things Frankie felt towards Vanya were unique enough to unnerve her. The only time she had felt anything like this was right before the bombing, when she was out clubbing with Lula and Jade. While hunting for some dumb himbo to impregnate her, she happened to see the most gorgeous girl in the smoking area. She had mousy brown hair and freckles all across her face. The girl couldn't stop looking at Frankie, and Frankie couldn't stop looking at the girl. Lula urged her to go and talk to her, so she did just that after downing a shot to calm her nerves.

When they got to the girl's flat, they made out, and then the girl put on an episode of *RuPaul's Drag Race*. They made out some more.

"Babe," said the girl between kisses. "Fuck me with your fingers, please."

On the screen, two queens glared at each other. Frankie's fingers worked their way up the girl's thighs while they continued to kiss. The girl had a curious habit: her kisses would start *active* and passionate and then quite suddenly she would stop, and all she would do is keep her mouth open as Frankie pushed her tongue further in. The saliva in the girl's mouth tasted like pure rum. Frankie touched her cunt, surprised at how wet it was, and at how wide it was too, a gaping mouth between the girl's slender thighs that seemed to suck her fingers in. It contracted as Frankie slid inside her. The girl moaned. Her shirt was open. Her tits were small, and Frankie kissed down her neck and on her breasts. She looked up and saw that the girl wasn't looking at her but at the TV, on which a drag queen twirled in a bright sequined dress. The girl didn't touch Frankie's body at all.

Soon after she came, the girl asked Frankie to leave, because she couldn't sleep with someone else in the same bed as her. It was four in the morning. Frankie had no money on her to get a cab, and when she tried to look at Uber it wouldn't load. She wasn't sure she knew this area. When she told the girl this, the girl just laughed and said, "Oh just head up the road over the hill and you'll be fine." Then, after a moment she said, "I hope you don't get killed. Stay sexy and don't get murdered."

Out in the dark night, the streetlights spread out in front of her. Frankie ran from pool of light to pool of light. Occasionally, one of the lamps would be dead, and there would be a wide empty gap where the ground was not visible. She hurried through the dark spaces. The road ahead sloped upwards and Frankie ran up the hill. It seemed, as she ran, that more and more streetlights were dead. The spots of illumination were scarce. When she found them, they made her feel safe, somewhat, although she knew this feeling was just a *trick of the light*.

When she stopped to get her breath back beneath one of these lamps, she saw a figure standing deathly still in a light pool on the other side of the road. She stood still too, for a moment, and then continued on her way. The figure didn't seem to move until she was a few houses past them. When she looked back, they were walking up the road, on the other side but in the same direction as her. She thought she saw a white bearded face. The only sound came from a couple of streets over – the screaming of a fox, which made her skin crawl all over with ghostly insectoid legs.

She turned off the road, off the planned route, but felt like the man was still there, even when she looked around and he wasn't. Just another girl walking home alone who wouldn't make it back. Another statistic. A dead trans woman whose name wouldn't be included when they released the yearly list of women murdered by men. It seemed so clear to her: the girl whom she'd had three fingers up to the knuckle inside not long before was in league with this man and had lured her out here, and this was the endgame. Get a tranny to make me cum before I let my boyfriend or Dad or boss or husband or bestie follow her home and corner her in a dark alleyway, or chase her into the green space called The Level, which is always lit at this time but never occupied apart from people so fucked out of their heads they wouldn't have anything to say to the cops when questioned. Chase her there, next to the skate park and the yellowing grass, and bend her over a concrete block and smash her head into it again and again while thrusting into her.

Frankie was walking as fast as she could now, no longer taking moments to get her bearings. She was convinced the man was just on a parallel street. *You're being paranoid. Calm down. I need to get home I need to get home.* There was no bus back to her house. She went up over the hill and back down it, feeling him at her heels, even when she turned and saw that he wasn't there. A couple of drunk girls were smoking on their balcony and called out something unintelligible to her. She glanced up at them, looking down on her like two angels haloed by the light through the screen door, angels pissed and high off weed, yes, but angels nevertheless. I'm scared, she called up at them. I think a man's following me. They descended to her on bright golden wings and lifted her up, until she was warm and nestled in the orange glow of heavenly safety. Well, one of them ran down and let her into their flat, stroked her hair. The other, the one on the balcony, looked for the man. Said she might have seen him on the other side of the street, saw a figure but wasn't sure. And Frankie could stay there if she needed, smoke some weed, sleep on the sofa. You are safe child, you are safe.

Frankie told this story once to someone, and they said, "Don't you think the way you talked about that girl's pussy was pretty misogynistic?"

~

"Oh shit!" Vanya came to a sudden halt.

The field they were in was, in contrast to the last few fields, recently shorn, probably by sheep. Vanya bent double and then, after a moment of looking at something on their thigh, they dropped down to sit on the grass, bending over so that their nose was practically touching their thigh.

"What is it?" called Frankie, catching up.

"I think I've got a tick."

From a few paces away, it looked like barely anything at all. Just a little red dot. When she got to Vanya's side, she sat down with them to look. It was still small, but it stood out against their pale skin. Buried in their flesh. The tick had found the only place on Vanya's entire body with enough meat to actually burrow down like that.

"You okay?"

Vanya nodded.

"Does it hurt?"

"A little bit," they said. "It's itchy. It didn't itch until I noticed it."

She spoke to them very firmly.

"Don't touch it."

"But it itches ..."

"Don't touch it!"

A sharp little intake of breath. "Okay. Okay."

"Do you have tweezers or something?"

"Yes. In my makeup bag, in my rucksack."

Their rucksack was a mess, but she found what she was looking for. Lots of the makeup in the bag seemed to be out of date or empty. She made a mental note to make them clean it all out. They looked hotter when they were boyish, anyway. The tweezers were right at the bottom. They didn't seem rusty, which was a miracle given how dirty it was in there.

She leaned down close to their thigh, until they could feel her breath on their skin. The tick was very still, but Vanya kept shivering. She told them to stop acting like a fucking baby. After she'd pulled it out, Vanya went suddenly tender. They asked if they could rest for a little while in the field, then they crawled into Frankie's arms and lay their head on her lap.

"I want to feel safe with you," Vanya said, half-asleep.

"Do you not feel safe?" Frankie asked.

But they had drifted off in her embrace. After she'd accidentally thrown them into the wall, a bruise had blossomed across their nose and their top lip. It had started to fade, gone from red to purple and now a light yellow. *Thank fuck, it was awkward being seen with them. Everyone wondering if it was me, all those dirty fucking looks.* She felt herself falling asleep too in the pleasant warmth of the sun, with the skylarks overhead screaming their little songs.

3

EMBARRASSING BODIES

You weren't to know, but your future lay down there in the bottom of that rancid bin. Flies swarmed and landed on the lollipop & became stuck there & died. Maggots were born beneath the rubbish; some lived their lives without ever seeing sunlight. It wasn't until you were fifteen that you were deflowered not by another person at all but by yourself. That summer was a scorcher, a record breaker said the woman on the news with a smile as old people everywhere were cooked in their cribs as the homeless struggled to find shade as public transport became unusable it was a scorcher, be sure to get down the beach and wear factor fifty was how she put it. Your parents worked during the summer your Dad was a plumber and your mother a care worker which later struck you as ironic because she never fucking cared for you not one inch not one iota. Your brother was two years older than you and he didn't have a girlfriend. That summer he made you wear your swimsuit and clean his bedroom for him when your parents were at work and he said don't tell them this or I'll shit in your bed so you didn't tell them and you kept doing it. He gave you pocket money for it this was how you first earned money this was your first and really your only job. But he was out one day the fateful day thank fucking God He was out. Your little sister was at some playscheme. Sometimes Mum asked you to look after her not that you had any talent for childcare you kind of just let her do whatever you couldn't be bothered to babysit. Mum regretted that, later on. But she was at a playscheme then thankfully. You lay on the living room sofa sweating like a pig. Lukewarm air blew from the pitiful fan you'd set up on the table next to the sofa every few seconds it would wash over you as it rotated first one way and then the other. The air wasn't really any cooler than the rest of the air but it was at least a change of pace. The television was on. Windows all open. Opposite your council house visible from the windows there was a little playpark sandwiched as it was between the two tenement blocks but it had been rusted for as long as you could remember as long as you'd lived there kids never played there the swing set was dangerous and the plastic slide covered in bird shit and the grass all around it dead. Now it was mostly used by older kids to go to later in the evening or at night or people sometimes met there to deal sometimes a student would come and pick up there students didn't live too far really only down the road but that might as well have been a different reality to the one you lived in. The council tried to put as much green space in the estate as they could but what was the use when shit was starting to fry apparently some boys a block or so away had lit their own patch of arid grass alight and the fire had spread to a wooden fence it had terrified people you'd caught the whiff of the smoke & people had thought one of the tower blocks might be burning when they found out it was grass it was almost disappointing. Under where you lounged on the chair was a dark wet patch of sweat you hadn't moved much for the last few hours really you only moved to get yourself a can of Coke not like real Coke supermarket coke it tasted weird and off but it was cool and sugary the television was on every five or so minutes you decided you were bored so you switched channel that was how you'd spent a good portion of the days that summer you didn't have friends and anyway who fucking wanted to play when it was like this outside you'd rather stay in and sometimes have to deal with Him than go out and get turned into dry dusty bones like the skull of a cow in an animation set in the Wild West. This would be a desert one day. This place. It would be consumed by a vast dune sea.

A bald man walked down a street that looked like yours. He wore a leather jacket and spoke directly to camera with an unearned cockney accent. Here on Scroungertown, we investigate some of the worst scroungers out there, people living it up on your hard-earned tax money. Cut to a woman with an innumerable number of chihuahuas barking. The bald man was now shown from behind, walking towards the woman. So, what makes you think this is fair, then? What makes you think this is acceptable? The woman coughed, and opened her mouth to defend herself, but the man kept going. Some people work for a living, you know, but here you are! Living it up with more dogs *than you can care for. Look at that TV! The camera panned to show the TV in the woman's living room. I'd guess it was a little larger than the one you were watching that very image on like only an inch or two wider but the irony was lost on you then and you don't even remember this detail now so there's no point in even focusing on it. The man turned to look at you through the screen. This woman is living fat and happy on your pounds. How does that feel? You clicked to the next channel. It wasn't even a new episode of* Scoungertown, *you'd seen that one before. Everything on every channel was a repeat. BBC Four was showing some old documentary about a man you didn't know called Benjamin Britten. UKTV Gold was playing some old sitcom about men working in an IT department. You weren't going to give up because you weren't looking for anything you weren't hunting this was all there was to do this was all British summertime had to offer you endless repeats they'd probably repeat the fucking 2012 Opening Ceremony soon it would be mandatory viewing remember when etc etc you were nearly asleep when you stumbled upon something that drew you out of your catatonia even if it was yet another repeat but it was a repeat of* Embarrassing Bodies *on one of those non-existent channels at the end of the line the ones that sit between the end of the real channels and the start of the porno ones. It had no place being shown during the day, before the watershed, but like who bothered to check things this far down the channel listing. You didn't yet have a moral conscience so you watched with passing interest about a woman with anal warts and a man with a micropenis a woman with a macroclit that sort of thing your clit was larger than you thought was normal but not as big as the one the woman had which was basically a cock the cock in your head twitched the malign pregnancy in some transsexual's bladder your period had just ended thankfully the flow had been heavy you thought you might be in trouble you still felt the ghost of pain oh, the sheer beautiful variety of the human body; its monstrous habit of causing difference, that was what this show investigated that was what it celebrated.*

A man named Henry had a problem. He was forty-six. He had recently been travelling abroad. When he came back he began losing weight, rapidly (Mum told you often you looked fat it's not baby fat you know because you're not a baby that's what she told you all the time) but Henry had been fat before and he was now losing weight very fast. They showed before pictures, and then they showed him shuffling into the Embarrassing Bodies *clinic in person, cloaked in clothes that swamped him he looked like a picture you'd seen of a sick gay man in the eighties ribcage visible as well as his spine. He didn't look like a man really he looked like an animatronic in a haunted house. Why the fuck was he even here? You couldn't even imagine the thought process as to why he didn't go to the NHS and instead went on this show were the wait times that bad even then that he'd let the camera ogle his body. The doctor said he had a parasite. Henry had eaten some raw fish so it seemed Henry had a tapeworm.* It might help with the weight loss *laughed the doctor* but it isn't generally recommended. *The man was put under anaesthetic. You were sad then when you realised they weren't going to show the extraction of the worm which surprised you really you didn't know that you'd been hoping they would show it but you could imagine what it might look like & that was good enough for the moment & then afterwards they did show the worm itself thank fuck and you touched yourself when they did you touched your cunt without really knowing you were doing it & the worm was still moving when they held it up in their forceps it was bewildered it had been comfortable fat and happy now it had been just like you were dragged into the disappointing light you could have cried but instead you came. Mum came back a little while afterwards. You didn't really understand what had happened there. Mum said it smelled bad in the room. Have you just been lying about farting all day? Then she sighed she left without another word. You liked the smell, though. The smell of shame sweat pleasure & pussy. You were waking up.*

4

SHIT-EATING GRIN

That summer was one for the records: scorching hot all day and uncomfortable at night too, even with every fan blasting and every window wide open. Frankie was a fucking idiot for working in an office with little to no ventilation. There was one air conditioner, but it was over the opposite side of the room to where her desk was, and she still had to dress at least semi-professionally. Some of the cis girls, such as Wolf, were getting away with having their thighs out, but she suspected she wouldn't be afforded that luxury.

She and Wolf had been hanging out during lunch breaks more. No, she didn't really like Wolf, but she didn't like any of her co-workers. Wolf at least had weed with her sometimes, even if talking to her could be disconcerting at times. Smoking weed with her out the back of the office block broke up the monotonous, soul-eroding cosmic bullshit of work.

The spot they went to was shaded, the building they worked in near-monolithic compared with everything else around. It blocked out the sun.

They were out there on the hottest day of the year so far. Frankie felt gross. It wasn't just the heat. Her heart was heavy with anxiety from the previous night with Vanya. Things had been going so well. The night was good and hot, but she'd made the stupid decision to bring up their living situation and the weird situation with their landlord. Was that all he was? The mere mention of him made her feel jealous, so she wanted to clear it up once and for all. They insisted that Gaz (that was his name, apparently) was a friend who was very kind to them. Frankie wouldn't have it. She pushed the subject further. The more they squirmed, the more convinced she was that something was up. No smoke without a fire. After a while, Frankie demanded to look at their phone.

Maybe it was a little too far. Vanya certainly thought so, at least initially. But she wore them down in the end. Nothing seemed to be on their phone, but that didn't mean she believed them. They offered to introduce the two of them. Frankie said "maybe". For the rest of the night, she was cold with them, even as they begged at her feet to be touched. The poor thing.

Wolf had just dyed her hair orange, a look that didn't suit her. She passed Frankie the blunt.

"You seem a bit off," Wolf said.

"Yeah."

"Wanna talk about it?"

Frankie did not. But the weed cheered her up a little. It stopped her mind from spinning so much. Wolf obviously thought she was upset about work, though, and used that as a springboard into talking about her favourite topic: whatever nasty shit she'd seen while working here. Frankie let her talk. It was too much effort to stop her anyway.

"This was actually before I worked here, but it was fucking *gross* ... So, I'm like a furry, right. I used to be a big deal, I guess because there weren't many hot cis girl furries back then, at least not visible ones. I was a big deal on like, Tumblr, and I fell into the orbit of this absolute *legend* furry guy who ... well, he was addicted to eating his own shit."

"Gross."

In the building's windows their respective bodies were warped nearly beyond recognition.

"It must have started as just a desire or something I suppose. He never said, but he must have been getting off on it to some extent. But by the time I knew of him, he was caught in this horrible cycle. He would try not to relapse. He'd be doing well – he'd post about how well he was doing. And then ..."

"Hmm."

"You can guess. He'd give in. Someone would egg him on, or he would look at some furry porn, and he'd relapse and eat his shit again. By the time I knew about him he must have been doing this long enough that he kept ending up in hospital with infections and shit from the scat-eating. The moment he got out, he would always be like, 'Okay, that was the last time I am never eating doodie EVER again,' a promise that everyone knew he'd break. And yeah. Then he broke it, went to hospital, came out, swore off the shit, ate it anyway, on and on and on. I ... as I said, some people egged him on. They got him to take pictures and videos by the end of it. I don't think any of us thought it would end. He seemed to enjoy it, so we were helping him out in a way. Removing his inhibitions. But then he was like, 'Oh God, the doctors told me that if I don't stop I'm going to die. They want to institutionalise me.' We called him a coward and told him he had to keep going. And then he posted a video of him chowing down on his shit, one last video. That was the last we heard from him. Someone found an obituary a little while later, and someone from the hospital who knew about the case leaked some of his details."

"Shit."

There was a long silence.

"I wouldn't have told you that if I wasn't high. I shouldn't have told you it. Sorry."

Wolf got up and headed back to her desk. She wouldn't look at Frankie for the rest of the day.

~

There was a billboard just about visible from Frankie's bedroom window advertising Absolut vodka. The billboard showed two trans women embracing and, at the bottom, the slogan "REACH YOUR ABSOLUT". The drinkaware.co.uk copy was incomprehensible, squashed down in the left-hand corner. Frankie could see it from her bed. Vanya was curled up next to her, but Frankie was still staring out the window at the advert. Sirens went past down the street. A drunk woman shouted at a drunk man on the pavement below, although the specifics of her grievance were dulled by distance and by her own alcohol consumption. Suddenly Vanya spoke.

"I'm really sorry about the other day. I shouldn't have resisted."

"That's fine," she said.

"I'd like you to meet Gaz. I think that would sort it out ... There is something I haven't told you, though."

Her grip on them tightened.

"What is it?"

"It's my birthday next week. I think we're going to have a party at the house. I'd like you to come."

"Why didn't you tell me that before?"

They shifted.

"I just forgot," they said, quietly. "That's all."

"You should have told me."

"I'm sorry ... Can you come though? It'll be on the Saturday."

She stopped cuddling them and sat up.

"Sure, I suppose I can."

"You can bring your friends if you like ..."

Lol. That wasn't going to happen. They weren't getting anywhere near Vanya. She wasn't going to let those cunts tear this thing apart.

~

Frankie kept forgetting to check her group chat with Lula and Jade. There had been no falling out, although the tension from the club night, while forgotten, was never actually resolved. She just looked at the messages often and told herself she'd reply when she could be arsed. That time never seemed to come. She didn't even message to tell them Vanya was now her partner.

Lula had dated a musician for a while who didn't let her post about him on her Instagram, supposedly because they were both *big online,* but the girls had worked out, through looking back through his account and his exes' accounts, that he had let them post about him as much as they wanted. It was pretty clear to everyone that he felt ashamed of Lula. Despite that, it was two more months before they broke up, and even then, he broke up with her. *The cunt.* That night though, unbeknownst to Frankie or to Jade, Lula was with him in his hotel room. He'd texted her at the last minute: *in town 4 a gig.* She hated herself for coming like a trained pet when he called. The linen hotel sheets were piled on the floor of the room and the room was a sauna. Jade texted her asking where she was, but she didn't answer until the following morning, when she claimed she had fallen asleep.

5

BINGE

It was another hot day & this was the summer of your discontent your summer of discontent where every day was the same but Mum & Dad were out again & He was out with his mates. He once told you He & His boys went to the woods to shoot squirrels with BB guns you didn't know if he was telling the truth or if he even had a BB gun he said without looking at you that if He shot you with one it would really hurt so what could you do. You had the run of the house a lot of days that summer. In the two nights since your Awakening you wanked constantly the cock in your head stiff you kept thinking about the worm being pulled out of him the way his body had collapsed in on itself the sunken eyes the sickness. You still had long hair back then that you wore tied up in the heat you snuck into your brother's room you went on his laptop the walls in his room were deep blue there were condoms on his bedside table you didn't have a laptop even though he had gotten this one when He was the same age as you Mum wouldn't let you have one there was lube on His bedside table a picture of a girl you came in here often it was unchanged but the floor was a mess he'd probably get you to tidy it the sick fuck but who are you to talk?

SEARCH: worst parasites found in humans.

[Most recent results first]

RESULTS:

QUEENSLAND WOMAN FINDS PARASITE IN EAR

A QUEENSLAND, AU. woman found that she had a parasite living in her ear canal. Susan Limbel, 46, began to complain of an incessant, loud scratching sound in her left ea ...

Q: IS THE STORY ABOUT SQUEEZING A SPOT AND LOADS OF BABY SPIDERS POPPING OUT TRUE?

Anon, there are no spiders known to lay their eggs inside of humans, so the urban legend is completely fictitio ...

TOP 5 WORST HUMAN PARASITES

It's never fun to think that your body might not be your own, but it's a fact of sc ...

SOUTH TEXAS WOMAN HAS 8 FOOT
TAPEWORM REMOVED FROM INTESTINE

A TEXAS woman was found to have an 8 FOOT
LONG tapeworm after she began to complain of
chronic stomach cramps. The worm was removed
by a team of surg ...

*Fuck her. That woman didn't know how good she had it. You
were jealous of the woman. Blessed by the universe & what had
she done? Just gotten it taken out? You wouldn't do that of course.
You'd never let them touch you. You'd cherish your parasite &
you wouldn't stop touching yourself not ever. Normal people
don't fantasise about this. You are so fucked up you thought ... A
bluebottle zipped past your head & slammed into the window it
fell onto the window sill lay on its back buzzing pathetically you
watched it passive you'd forgotten what you were thinking about.*

SEARCH: want to have a tapeworm? [Most recent
results first]

Eating Disorder Discussion Forum: I NEED TO
GET A FUCKING TAPEWORM ALREADY I HATE
MYSELF IT'S THE ONLY WAY

surely the only way I could ever lose weight
because Im such a useless fat fuck Im too lazy to
exercise I just want something else to eat all my
fucking calories away I'm serious like I dsont care
how ill it makes me it's the only way otherwise I'll

just keep binging and restricting and Im stuck in the cycle does anyone know how I can get eggs or if theres any bad sushi restaurants in London I can go to that will give me some (is that rac ist its just idk I cant think anyway)

I tried it … it worked .,.. at least until I collapsed and they removed it at the hospitalWITHOUT MY CONSENT eyeroll

WHERE DID YOU GET IT FROM TELL ME RN IM FUCKING DESPERATE I'LL KILL MYSELF IF I DOINT GET A TAPEWORM

WHY ARENT YOU ANSWERING BITCH? BITCH MY DEATH WILL BE ON YOUR HANDS

Calm down gurrrl I got them here … bt.lx.ru

The posts were from a while ago. You might well have been reading the words of ghosts. The link in the last reply no longer worked now all it led to was some Russian porn website the top video some emaciated girl being fucked up the arsehole by a big dicked white guy which wasn't really your sort of thing was it? You opened Yahoo Answers & wrote out a question: I think I'm turned on by the idea of having a tapeworm? Is this normal? You sent it before you could second guess yourself & you didn't want to push your luck by staying in His room much longer so you deleted the day's browsing history you saw that last night He had looked at teen stepsister pornography he'd be home soon he came home soon the next day when he was out again you went back to see if there had been any answers. There were six but four told you to kill yourself one was a spam account even you could tell that but the last the last the last: It isn't normal, no *it said.* But you aren't alone. There's quite a few people who feel the same thing, or similar. You should consider checking out our forum if you like – it's called infested4ever.com. You have to fill out a form to apply for an account, but just answer as honestly as you can.

6

THE PLACE BEYOND

Frankie guessed that whoever this Gaz was, he was the sort of rich person whose relationship to money was more abstract than it was material. Despite knowing that, she wasn't prepared for how *fucking huge* his house was going to be in real life. Vanya said they wanted to solve this issue, make it clear she had nothing to worry about when it came to Gaz. It didn't feel like that. It felt like they were rubbing her face in shit.

She stood at the bottom of the stairs that led up to the front door. The house glowered down at her, asking her what she was doing here, she was far too poor to be allowed here. A posh terraced house, a four-walled box containing all the blood and guts implied by its own existence. *Frankie, you don't belong here. Just turn around. Just go home.* With every step up closer to the door, she felt the tension inside her grow. But giving up would make her some sort of coward. She wasn't going to lose to some posh cunt who called himself Gaz. She was at the front door now, so shiny and black that she could just about see her own face reflected in the well-varnished paint. That varnish looked fresh. Vanya's work, she suspected. *Gaz* probably made them do all that kind of work.

Frankie wore her nicest black dress. She even wore heels. Noise from the party leaked out from the house, but no neighbours seemed to be mad. No neighbours even seemed to be there. In the whole crescent, it was only this house that showed life. Every other window was dark. For all she knew, the whole world could be cloaked now in night. This house might be the last bastion of light left, and if it was then the world was doomed, because there was something very bad here. There was something so purely unwelcoming, unhomely, about its monstrous *poshness*. A place so far from Frankie's self that entering its boundaries might cancel out her existence.

She texted Vanya that she was outside and soon they came to her. The door opened, they hugged her, and they beckoned her in.

"God, you look so hot," they said when they saw her.

I should run away. I should get the fuck out of here.

"Happy birthday, Vanya," she said as she kissed their neck, their ear, their mouth.

"Come inside, now. I want you to come inside."

"I can't wait to fuck you later." Hearing that, she felt their body, embraced in her arms, spasm with excitement. And they pulled her into her house. What was she going to do ... break free and run away? No. She let herself be pulled deeper. *Stupid slut. If this goes bad then you deserve it ... When this goes bad then you'll have deserved it.*

~

Frankie's present to Vanya was a metal collar: a stainless-steel ring to wear around their neck with another, smaller ring hanging from the front. A loop, to which a lead or chain might be attached. They looked wonderful in it when she put it on them. It was just a tiny bit too tight. Not tight enough to choke them, but tight enough to be *slightly* uncomfortable. Like fingers applying gentle pressure to the throat. It looked cute!

Now Vanya was wearing their gift, they walked down the house's entrance hall. Frankie felt odd being led along by them, so she put her hand on their arse as they went together, just to make sure they knew their place.

"It's through here," they said. There was a door at the end of the corridor that opened out into the living room, which was less of a living room and more of some kind of hall. Despite its size, people were packed in, barely able to dance but dancing anyway, beneath, absurdly, a *glitter ball*. It was kitschy, far too kitschy for her taste. But maybe this was who they were when they weren't around her. As the two of them weaved through the crowd, people smiled at them, wished them happy birthday, stroked their shoulders in greeting. Frankie squeezed their bum just a little tighter. Ugly music blared from the speakers. Some blonde twink stood at a deck on the other side of the room, twiddling knobs that Frankie was sure did nothing. She hated this shit. It was unlikely that Vanya knew all these people, and she wouldn't have believed it if she wasn't seeing the way everybody smiled at them.

Out through the back door the sun had nearly gone down and the sky was bloody. Some people lay together on the grass in an embrace, gazing up with ridiculously wide pupils at the sky. Frankie couldn't begin to imagine what it was they could see up there.

"My housemates are just out here," Vanya said. "Or at least they were the last time I checked ..."

"Gaz too?"

"Yeah. He should be out here."

The garden stretched back further than Frankie expected. Having a garden this size in the middle of a city was absurd, but it seemed *Gaz* did. They crossed the lawn and through a layer of bushes. There were trees now, decorated with fairy lights. They were small trees, but still ... trees in a city garden.

"Ah," Vanya called. "Hey you lot!"

Four figures sat under one of the trees turned as one towards them.

"It's wild in there," said one of the figures. He had the voice of a posh boy. *So, is this Gaz?* He didn't look like much to her. When he stood up and walked closer, she took stock of his height: shorter than her, just about. With his freshly shaved head, he looked a little like Ewan McGregor in *Trainspotting*, which made the poshness of his voice sound even sillier.

"It seemed fun," said Frankie.

"Oh it is, I just hope they don't destroy my house too much."

Vanya coughed. "This is Frankie, Gaz. My ... the girl I've been dating."

Frankie put her arm around them.

"Hi, Gaz," she said, and smiled what she hoped was her friendliest smile. She suspected it didn't look much like that.

"Hello, Francesca."

What a smarmy grin he had. What a weak handshake too. She shook his hand when offered but having to make contact with his palm, with his long, skeletal fingers, could have made her gag. It baffled her. *This* guy was the guy who told Vanya what to do, the guy she felt so jealous of? He was *nothing*, he was less than nothing. Maybe it really was just about money and class. That sort of thing could make up for a lot. She ought to slap him right now, but she'd promised to be nice, or at least try to be. So, she sat down, arm still wrapped around Vanya.

"We've heard a *lot* about you," said one of their other housemates in between clouds of sugary vape. Vanya introduced them as Judith.

"Good stuff, I hope." *Clichéd-arse line.*

"Mostly," smiled Judith.

"Mostly," agreed another. Vanya told her who the others were, the one who had just spoken and the one sat with them: Tyler and Hyron, both punks with fake-leather jackets draped over their shoulders. Frankie got the impression that they wore those jackets whatever the weather, no matter the occasion. Hyron had white-person dreads.

"Vanya's a very special person," said Gaz. "So, we've been curious to meet you. Sorry if there's a meet-the-parents vibe, *lol*."

She felt hot, even if they were outside. "It is a little like that. I promise I'm just a normal girl."

They sat and chatted. It was awkward at first, but it felt easier as she talked to them more. *They're just nervous, it's fine*, she told herself. *Vanya wants this to work so make it work and don't get too controlling.*

She heard a bang from back in the house. "Don't you want to make sure they don't trash your place?"

Gaz shrugged.

"It's not really *my* house ..."

Vanya giggled. "No, it's your Dad's."

He shrugged. "Well, do any of us really *own* anything ... Sorry, that was a joke. Couldn't resist it. Yeah, my Dad technically owns it. He owns this whole block. I know. You don't have to say it, I know what you're thinking."

Vanya chipped in. "I'd usually hate rich people, but Gaz like ... takes what he's been lucky enough to be handed and uses it for good, you know. He got this house, and he used it to make a little commune."

"Are you an anarchist?" Frankie asked him, not that she knew the first thing about anarchism.

"Hyron and Tyler are," Gaz said. "I wouldn't say I am. I suppose I'm an accelerationist."

Hyron rolled their eyes. "I'll never understand that shit. Don't tell me you're one as well, Frankie?"

"Oh ... no, no. I'm not anything."

"Well, you should be something. The world's gonna burn soon ... don't you care about nature?"

Frankie shrugged.

"That's what we should be modelling ourselves on, man ... There are things in the woods that no living person has seen, same as in the ocean, same as in the caves. There is another country beneath this one, or inside this one, or in exactly the same place as this one, only slightly out of sync. Beyond this one. Another place. If you get fucked up enough, you can see it."

That last sentence caught her interest. "Can you see it right now?"

"Not that fucked up yet," said Hyron. "Maybe later."

"I do have a good selection of drugs," winked Gaz. "If that's your sort of thing, Frankie. Come on, let's go inside and dance."

7

INCUBATION

You lied on the website application form by saying you were a nineteen-year-old girl named Vee who lived in London. Obviously you were a better liar than you thought because they believed you they let you in either that or the person who reviewed applications didn't actually care they might have just let everyone in this was something that only occurred to you after the fact at the time you believed in your own ability to tell a fib you constructed Vee as a person distinct from yourself Vee was not the same as Vanya they were a different person and I'll tell you a secret now but you have to promise not to tell anyone else okay are you prepared well You are a different person from Vanya. You are legally distinct. But that next week your brother was home alone a lot he'd gotten into a fight with one of his boys so you couldn't look at the website any more you only went into his room when he told you to.

BRAINWYRMS

When he did go out finally & you made it on you calmed. It wasn't just a forum for people who wanted to have tapeworms, it was for people who were sexually excited by the idea of parasites. Some of these people wanted to have parasites, some of them wanted to give other people parasites, and some of them liked the idea of both of those things. When you made it on that day the top post was titled 'progress'. You clicked on it you were overjoyed & paranoid He might walk in but fuck was it worth it see because the post was accompanied by an image of the user's amazing-looking tits small hard nipples some arteries were faintly visible through pale skin good tits not excessively large good tits very round & perky but it wasn't any of that which made you squeal it was the inflamed lump positioned next to the nipple on the left tit an inflamed red lump with a bulging head filled with pus. If I'm correct and if everything has worked how I hoped, there should be a botfly larvae incubating inside this bad boy lol. *God did you want to kiss those tits. God did you want to kiss that lump. You told her that in the comments under the post & she thanked you.*

8

COKE

Frankie's dress was too fucking tight. The mirror hanging on the wall showed her it was too tight, *visibly* too tight. She had done a shit job of shaving her legs. Her shoulders in the dress looked manly. She needed lipodissolve in her chin. Her breasts didn't look like the breasts of a woman, they looked like the breasts of a man abusing steroids. Like Meat Loaf's tits in *Fight Club* ... that was it. *I look like that,* she thought. *I look like Meat Loaf in* Fight Club *and everyone here thinks that too, everyone... everyone...*

Vanya kissed her, and the train of thought was destroyed. Perhaps they couldn't even see any of those things. Perhaps they didn't care. They liked her, right? They liked her, or they wouldn't kiss her. Hundreds of points of pink light reflected from the glitter ball and brushed over their handsome face. They handed her the bag and the key.

A shirtless twink, a different one, she thought, from the one who had been DJing, stood on one of the sofas. He screamed when the song changed. Frankie couldn't work out if the screaming was supposed to be positive or negative. The twink might not have known either. Streamers drifted like cobwebs through the air. A girl was being fingered in the corner.

She did two bumps of coke. It had been quite a while since she'd done any. When you don't take coke for a while it's easy to forget how bad the chemical taste at the back of your throat can get. When the taste suddenly appeared, she thought she might vomit, but Vanya held her hand and gave her water until it went away. She felt vulnerable. It was wrong. It was all wrong, but she let them soothe her anyway.

The coke was rich-people coke. She hadn't had that kind of coke in a long time, had forgotten how it might as well have been a different drug entirely from the cocaine she usually took. It was sharper. It didn't make her head throb with pain. It was a real hit, a pick-me-up. No fucking flour here, no cutting with lesser drugs or whatever they had lying around. This was the real pure shit. She could practically taste the labour of the Colombian kids who made it.

The crowd was starting to thin out now, just a little bit. All the normies were off. There were still enough people in the living room that it felt like a crowd, that it almost seemed a little dangerous. She took some more coke. What else was there to do? Over on the other side of the room Gaz was kissing some girl she didn't recognise.

She pulled Vanya closer to her by the collar. The sexual excitement flashed over their face.

"I'm going to fucking destroy you," she muttered in their ear, unsure if they even heard her.

9

A TRUE STORY

You began to tell them stories. The other night my Mum was watching a nature show, and there was a segment about a parasite that looked like a giant pillbug. It ate fish's tongues and then replaced them in the fish's mouth, and the fish never knew the difference. There was footage of a fish with its mouth gaping open wide and a little thing in there, in place of where the tongue should be, two black eyes peering out. I know it would never eat a human's tongue, I know enough about biology to know that but ... fuuuuuck. Imagine how amazing that would be, walking around with a creature in your mouth? I had to go to bed early that night if you know what I mean. My pussy was so wet, and I couldn't stop thinking about letting something crawl into my mouth and devour my tongue ... taking away my ability to speak, taste, anything, and replacing it with itself. I'd be able to feel it constantly, its little legs against the bottom of my mouth, its carapace against the top. I shoved my face into my pillow to stop my screams from waking everyone in the house. *They loved the stories you told. You kept telling them until you were spent, and then you made up more.*

10

SWEET SYRUP, SWEET NECTAR

"Where's Vanya?" Frankie called to Gaz. He didn't hear her, or at least he didn't react. The clock on the wall had the wrong time: it said it was only nine, but when she checked her phone it was three am.

Time was different in this house. It hadn't been that long since she arrived, but it had been an eternity. She stumbled in Gaz's direction, right up to him. He wasn't with that girl now, he just stood alone. Like he was waiting for her to approach.

"Where's Vanya?"

"They're waiting for you, Francesca," he said.

"Oh ... What?"

"They're waiting for you. In their bedroom. They want you to go to them, I think."

"Which room is theirs'?" she asked, but Gaz ignored her question. Instead, he stood up and pressed a large clear bottle of dark brown liquid into her hands.

"They just had some of this. You should drink some too. Really enhances the vibe."

The bottle that she held didn't have a label. Its contents looked to her like syrup. "What is it?"

"Homebrew." He leaned in and in a conspiratorial stage-whisper he said, "I brew it in the basement. Don't tell anyone."

"Will it wake me up, though? I'm flagging."

"Oh yeah. It'll put some fire in you."

It tasted sugary at first, but there was an unpleasant after-taste of bitterness that made her cough.

Gaz chuckled and snatched the bottle back. "Top of the main stairs, go right, and then it's the room next to the toilet."

"What?"

"Vanya's room! Keep up."

"Oh," she said. The floor was uneven. "Thanks."

"They're waiting for you."

"Thank you." She turned away from him.

"Fat tranny," he said, matter-of-factly.

"What?" She turned back.

"I said I think they're horny."

"That wasn't what you said, though."

"Yes it was. Have fun."

Gaz gently pushed her in the right direction, and she began to hurry. Top of the stairs, next to the toilet ... Fat tranny. *Fat tranny, Meat Loaf, fat tranny* ... God, that stuff he'd given her was weird. Fly Agaric wine, maybe ... but it tasted sweet, not bitter, not sweetbitter, but sweet. People were still dancing, even on the stairs. Three AM. Fat fuck. Dress splitting. No, no. Vanya was waiting for her. She nearly stumbled on the steps as she tried to take two, three at once.

Vanya. Fuck. She wanted to fuck them so badly. She felt hard already, she hoped that nobody could see her cock poking through her dress. When she tried to readjust its position to make it less visible, there wasn't a cock there at all, and she remembered that she didn't have one anymore. For a moment, though, she had been so sure of the sensation of an erection that she could have sworn it was real. *I'm coming for you Vanya I hope you're ready to get fucked I'm coming for you I'm coming for you I'm a f ...* She could see the door she thought Gaz meant and she pushed it open. Vanya was there, naked as Adam, glowing softly in the light of six or so candles scattered throughout the room. Frankie barrelled over their floordrobe, desperate to get them in her arms.

"I was wondering if you were ever going to come find me," they said, their fingers between their thighs. Stroking.

11

NONBINARY

You had a message.

Hello Vee. Ur new?

Yes im new! Whats ur name?

G. ive been on here for like 3 years now

Woah

Are you a boy or a girl?

To be fair you had been thinking variations on the same thing you didn't feel like what you imagined a little girl might/ could/should feel like you felt like something else but in the mirror even though you wore no makeup and you rarely wore skirts you saw a girl the person in the mirror they looked like a girl but a girl wouldn't do this would they you wished you didn't have to make any decisions you wished you had no agency you wanted to be a host to things not a thing yourself.

Not sure Im a girl but sometimes im a bit like a boy.

Oh so like nonbinary? Cool. Look this website is cool but not easy to use to talk. Do u have a phone? Ur in the UK right so wont get loads of charges n stuff ☺

I have a phone, ye. Heres my number

Then, later, when you had lost hope that he might text you: hi Vee. Its G from the forum.. obvs my name isn't really G. its Gaz. I shouldn't really tell you that but anyway it was good chatting thank you for trusting me with your number.

My name's Vanya *you said. You're not meant to tell people online your real name but you said it anyway.* I'd love to chat some more.

12

FILTH

"Mummy?"

"That's right, that's right. Call me that again," she said.

"*Mummy* ... Oh God, *Mummy*."

"It's your birthday, so Mummy's got a little treat for her little whore."

The way they looked at her ... those eyes, wet. Their face flushed red from being hit.

"But if you want it, first you have to do something for Mummy. You have to pretend to be a boy, you have to pretend you're fucking her, okay?"

They looked confused.

"Fuck, I'll just ride you, alright? Pretend you've got a cock and you're fucking me with it. It's just a thing I want, don't fucking question."

"... Okay ... I just ... It makes me feel a bit weird, pretending to have a dick. Like, dysphoric."

She felt hot. It wasn't that hard to just pretend, surely. "Just do it for me. I just need it."

"Um ... fine," they said.

Fine. Not "Yes of course, Mummy." Not "I'd love to." Just ... *fine.* But she got on top of them, anyway. And she pretended, for a moment, that they really did have a cock that could shoot up inside her, fill her up with cum until she was bursting. It felt pretty wonderful to imagine, and by the end they were smiling too.

"Time for your gift, for being such a good boy," she said when she was satisfied.

Frankie kissed their face and down their neck. Whatever Gaz had given her was hitting hard. She kissed their naked little breasts and bit their small hard nipples and she kissed down their body, the thin skin of their ribs and their concave stomach. Their skin was greyer than it should have been, but from under it she felt a burning heat, reassuring her once again that she wasn't a necrophile. She kissed their hips, the nothing of their thighs.

"Yes, Mummy, please ... please, Mummy..."

The distant memory of an idea floated in her head. She had wanted to see Vanya's bedroom. It had been kept from her for so long that the idea of it had become mythic. But now the room was just a pink and white blur. All she could focus on was their body. Those colours bled into one another, the pink sheets bled onto their skin, the skin bled into the walls. Like a watercolour painting, ruined. Vanya dug their nails into her and she felt real again. The blurriness ceased. On their bedside table she spied a copy of Mark Fisher's *Ghosts of My Life*.

Who are you? Really? Vanya? Who are you? I don't know you at all. But she kept on kissing their thighs because they begged her to, and because it felt so good to hear their moaning.

"I want to make you cum."

"Make me cum, Mummy," they gasped. Their cunt tasted sour, like fermenting fruit. That was the first thing that struck her. The initial taste wasn't unpleasant, exactly, but it was unexpected. They were very wet and very warm down there. She licked it more with her eyes shut because the colours still hurt her head. The sour, fizzy taste masked another taste, a putrid one. Involuntarily, Frankie gagged. Something was in her mouth. She gagged again and withdrew in a panic.

"What's wrong?"

Vanya sat up to look at her. "Do you feel sick? Was it the coke?"

It wasn't the coke. Frankie didn't look at their face. She was staring at their cunt. Their pubic hair was very dark, their pussy was bright red. And from the lips of their cunt dangled worms. It was the worms she stared at, trying to determine if they were real, and *if* they were real, how she should act. The worms were about the length of an index finger, and as she watched, one dropped right out of Vanya, landing on the bedsheet with a quiet squelch. She opened her mouth to say *worms*, but that was when she felt the thing in her mouth move. The worm on the bed flailed in panic. She spat the one in her mouth onto the floor as she ran from the room, but even with it gone the rotten taste was still there. Oh how she gagged and coughed and spluttered and gasped her way out of the bedroom, leaving Vanya confused and hurt in her wake.

They were inside her now, the worms. Her stomach was a living knot of them. She clutched herself, she could feel a horde of them filling up her organs, more and more with every moment. If she didn't expel them her insides would burst. From behind her she heard Vanya calling, but it was no use telling them what was happening to her. Any delay would mean the worst possible outcome. The bathroom, the fucking bathroom, was next door to their bedroom. It was the white door; it was right there. Something in her stomach gurgled and she retched suddenly and dryly, which caused her to stumble, which caused her to lose a precious second. Thank fuck the bathroom wasn't occupied. She slammed the lock behind her. It was an off-colour dirty white in there, covered in stray bits of hair and limescale. The sink had yellow rings around its inside. She gagged again once she was bent over it. It was just in time, because the retching wasn't dry anymore. She threw up a wash of foul-tasting liquid, and in the liquid there were worms. Each worm landed on the ceramic with disgusting wet slaps. Was that it? Her head spun madly. *In through the nose, out through the mouth, in through the nose, out through the mouth ...* She followed those instructions, but soon more vomit bubbled its way up her throat, and with the vomit came more worms. Not just a few this time: far too many to count surged out of her mouth with each gag until her knees were shaking and she was sobbing, and then there were even more. She was bent double. *Back arched like a fucking slut.*

In the sink, the worms struggled to find any purchase, and became tangled in one another. Somebody – Vanya? Gaz? – banged a fist on the door with some urgency.

"Fuck off," she tried to say, but it came out as nothing more than a wet gurgling. With each gag her whole body tensed up, and after each gag the release she felt was nearly beautiful. It never lasted very long. Lightness. Her body could have levitated, her head could have reached heaven. Then she was dragged back down to earth, to the scummy tiles, the limestone, another round of vomiting up everything she'd drunk or eaten, another round of spitting out the worms. The bathroom had smelled ambiently bad before, the smell of a bathroom in a house where lots of young people live. But now just the stink of the air would have been enough to make anybody else throw up too. The stench of half-digested food and curdled alcohol mixed with stomach acid, and of course the sour–sweet rotting smell of the worms. It made her head spin; she could have gotten high from it.

13

DEFLOWERING

He was nice to you. Really it was that simple that was all it took for you to get groomed by him. You were young & scared you were convinced there was something very very wrong with you your brother and your mother you were horny confused failing school && he listened to you you were in his thrall you'd have done anything he told you to but mostly he didn't even tell you to touch yourself or send him pics or stuff like that mostly he just said you didn't deserve the abuse. But when he did sext you loved it didn't you? It took you apart to pieces it took you to pieces he said:

Thinking abt your cute body in agony bc you have a blood fluke infection ... did u know they can make you infertile if left untreated?? You cant rlly see them bc theyre tiny but they're so cool looking

Pls give me them Im thinking abt it abt the pain and how id struggle peeing aaaa

But before long the everyday pain of horniness got too much you were like fuck you needed to actually experience something just reading and looking and dreaming it wasn't good enough on the forum you asked people if they could refer to you with they/ them pronouns refer to them with they/them pronouns. People were mostly nice about it. Some complained about SJWs taking over the forum but like who cares fucking boomers. A lot of people think of the internet as a vast lake it's deep, dark, frequently difficult to navigate there are things at the bottom which have been long forgotten about but if someone has a particular niche fetish and the internet is the primary source by which this person accesses content related to that fetish, it is not vast at all. In fact, for them, it's tiny. It's the same ten or so things reposted over and over again. Sure, the lake is huge, but there is a particular type of fish that lives in its depths, and that type of fish is rare. Think of the fetishist as a freshwater fisherman. That was the problem you came across quite quickly. You couldn't cope. You had to do it. You told Gaz you had to do something He said well it's a rite of passage. You asked what you should do you needed to stop being a coward really you were fucked in the head your brother said you had a dick in your brain your Mum complained about an article in the paper about pronouns your brother left his bottle of lube by the side of your bed your father got punched by a guy at work no one could ever understand the type of stress you were under.

I need you to tell me what to do gaz I need yoju to tell me what to do I cant cope with this fucking place you don't know how bad they are theyre evil tell me what to doi please

Do you live in an area with foxes?

Tell me to do it.

R u sure

I'm sure tell me to do it

God your so hot

Tell me to do it

Ok here's what you have to do

& then he told you what to do & you listened patiently carefully & then once he had told you what to do you did it. You did what he told you to do.

YOU [that is, the reader, not the character] are welcome to take a break here given the extremity of the content explored in the next series of chapters. It isn't shameful to take a break. It is in fact encouraged that you do so right here, so that this novel does not become

overwhelming to you. Take a break, get
a cup of tea or some water. Maybe go for
a walk. Then come back and continue
reading, safe in the knowledge that you
[the reader] have fortified your consti-
tution and thus can handle what follows.

You [the character, not the reader] *crept out of your parent's
house that night phone in one hand used as a blaring torch
lighting your way key in the pocket of your coat you wore
pyjamas under it you wore slippers on your feet also in the
pocket of your coat a handful of supermarket plastic bags &
when you closed the door you eased it shut so it barely made any
noise at all.*

*Outside the streetlights bathed everything in an orange glow that
made nothing feel real. You may as well have been dreaming.
Were you dreaming? This wasn't where you lived it was a sepia
film of it & you walked through that sepia film the dull light of the
streetlights the older teens in the park huddled about the tower
blocks in the starless sky with windows that glowed & in some
of them silhouettes of figures moved around or stood very still as
if they were abandoned shadow puppets. You saw foxes you saw
cats domestic & feral in the night outside what difference could
there be you went left down the street past all the parked cars the
houses that looked identical to your own they built this place fast
they built it cheap the houses were brittle. Dad said he could do*

a better job but they wouldn't let him fix it because it would void the damage deposit.

What followed was mythic it had the feeling of a story: a dead fox guts steaming on the hot tarmac entrails forming a crude arrow for you to follow your spirit guide it guided you to a pile of shit on the pavement freshly made by this very same fox before it lost its life to a car already flies were swarming around the corpse & the shit. This is a story you said to yourself. This isn't real. I am in a twilight world. But it was real of course it was real you knew that too you were glad of it the shit was still warm when you picked it up in the plastic bag. It was still warm when you carried it in the plastic Tesco bag to an alleyway twixt two houses. It had been quite solid when you picked it up the surface already had gone crusty but now it was softening in the airless bag a fly was trapped in there buzzing too the alleyway was dark no one around you were in a twilit world you had crossed over to another place beyond a place only you knew about & you were ready you couldn't hesitate it was time you needed to do this before you got too scared & chickened out so you propped your phone up against the opposite wall. There was a puddle on the uneven floor of the alleyway a puddle of spilled curdled milk. The torch light coming out of your phone made your crotch glow. You had taken off your pyjamas and your coat already. You pulled a handful of shit out of the bag. The fly had died. One of the same flies that stuck to your lollipop, the same fly that hit the window next to you when you had been sat in your brother's room always the same fly. The shit felt strange in your hand but what had you expected it to feel like?

BRAINWYRMS

No time for caution. You shoved it inside yourself. It was wet hot it was sharp it spread up from your cunt to your torso the feeling you gagged you hated that you did that it stunk you pushed it as far as it would go then you got more from the bag and shoved that in as well then you masturbated you squirted when you climaxed brown liquid came out of you onto your thighs.

When you returned to your bed you told him you'd done it. He said you were a good boy.

14

ARSEHOLE

Ah, she thought. *I see clearly. I see it now. I'm just a fucking hole.* She wiped her tears away with the back of her hand. The light above her flickered. With each flash it made a sound. Something inside of the bulb sparked. But despite that, despite the foul smell, despite Vanya knocking insistently on the other side of the door, she felt better than she had all evening. There was a pair of nail scissors lying on the sink next to the pot of toothbrushes. Frankie picked them up and pressed one of the blades into the underside of her wrist until it began to feel like something. The scissors were blunt, they didn't cut her. Unfortunately. She dropped them on the floor.

"Frankie please open up," said Vanya on the other side of the door. She didn't like it. It disturbed her peace. "Do you need us to call an ambulance?"

"Fuck off," she shouted.

"Frankie?"

"Just ... stop talking. You put fucking *things* inside me. I'm infected. You're disgusting, you disgust me." Her stomach felt completely empty now, though it still throbbed.

They stopped. She heard a sniffle.

"Are you *crying?* Fucking pathetic. You need to wash yourself more often, you're crawling with things. You stink like rotten meat."

In the sink the worms slowly ceased their writhing. Soon they would probably be dead. They were not equipped for life outside of her body. Devoid of her life-giving fluids, they were going to dry out. In the summer, after rain, the worms that came up out of the earth became confused and got scorched to death on the pavement. The light above her, the strip light, flickered. *Don't you give up on me. Don't leave me in the dark.* Her mouth was parched. She turned on the cold tap and drank from it. The water washed some of the worms at the bottom of the sink down the plughole, but there were so many that soon it ended up blocked. She turned the tap off again and punched the wall. The pain was good. Her knuckles bled. The strip light flickered. Vanya, crying outside the door. The taste of their cunt still on her tongue. If she believed in something then she could have prayed, but she believed in nothing, no god or creed, no ideology beyond survival. The world was a frightening place; it was better to believe in something. Hope could be found, or solace. Hope for the world or solace that it was doomed.

She could feel a pressure in her gut.

Ah, fuck, she thought. It wasn't over. They were still in her body. Perhaps they always would be. It was an emergency. There was no longer time to think about what it meant. If she didn't get onto the toilet immediately, she was going to shit herself. It was strange how that happened: one moment you became aware of the need to shit, and the next you absolutely *had* to shit *right then* or else. The toilet was gross. It didn't look like it had been cleaned in months. Vanya had been slacking. Or, more likely, Gaz didn't ask them to clean at all. He made them do other things, and they did them willingly.

Vanya's voice came again. "Frankie? I don't … I don't understand."

"Are you so fucking *retarded* that you can't understand two simple words? *Fuck! Off!*"

Silence.

The dress, the stupid fucking tight dress, she was too big for it, and she couldn't pull it over her thighs. *Fuck, fuck.* She pulled at the hem, but it wouldn't shift. It dug into the flesh of her thighs so deep that they were compressed. It was taking all the strength she had to keep her asshole shut. Eventually, she just ripped the dress open and tore off her panties. Not a moment too soon. The toilet seat was freezing on her bare arse cheeks. She tried to stare up at that flickering light. It made her head split. The blurriness was back again, the white of the walls began to ripple all around her. Eyes from far off observed her with interest. They looked down at her debasing herself, and with great cosmic mouths filled with great sharp cosmic teeth and long tongues, they chuckled at her. They were out there somewhere in the distance. Get fucked up enough and you can see them. She screamed, she sobbed, she pleaded for mercy as she shat out worms. The only sound was that of the worms splattering into the water at the bottom of the toilet bowl, worm after worm after worm. Some guy somewhere online would probably pay more money than Frankie had ever seen in her life just to watch this happen, but she was doing it for free and to no audience. Loser.

The smell of her shit, of the gases coming out of her asshole, of all of it, mixed with the smell of her vomit, mixed with the ambient grossness of the bathroom. She gagged again. It would never end, would it? Fart, shit, throw up, shit, cry. Her nails in the palms of her hands. The scissors, rubbish as they were, would have been something but they were too far out of reach for her now. The light gave out, and she was left on her own in that awful place.

In the past, Vanya shoved the shit inside themselves. Then, later, Frankie pushed it out. Through elastic time, they inverted one another.

15

AGONY

*Itchy ... itchy ... it itched ... The next day it was so itchy you tore
your skin itchy it went all red raw you didn't tell your parents it
itched yet this was good this meant it was working you said* it
itches *to Gaz he said* that's good *the next day it was sore the
next day you were in agony you wanked in your room and in your
squirt this time you thought you could see little clear worms next
day there was yellow discharge the colour of snot you struggled
to walk you fell down the stairs and hit your head Mum saw took
you to hospital you started screaming the doctors were baffled
they made you take antibiotics you tried to throw them up you
tried to run they caught you you tried to kill yourself they stopped
you you didn't want a body you wanted to die you didn't want a
body you wanted to cum when you recovered you told Gaz and
he said he would take you away & save you. Then you informed
him of something you hadn't ever told anybody about before.* 1

said my brother was rough and horrible... well I guess it's not just that. He touches me sometimes. He's been doing it for a while. I'm scared of him.

You met Gaz on the beach you drank from a bottle he brought along with him. It was starting to get chilly in the evening now so you huddled together. He told you about his life and his perspective he said for him this wasn't just a fetish this was a life see and you understood. People take fetish and kink seriously, they treat it as a lifestyle and structure their existence around it. There are many people in communities on the internet who essentially are engaged in fetish that would never think of it as such. There are communities of men online who obsess over cigars, their phallic shapes, the feeling of having them in their mouths, and they may never realise what that really means. They might never even get off on it properly. There are communities of people who dress up in Red Army costumes who don't fuck one another – and yet ... fetishes can burst out of the specific easy boundaries they are put in and overcome the entire self. They can become an ideology. A lot of people live like this. Gaz was one of them. It was not enough to simply get infected. It couldn't just be that. It had to be something more. It had to have some wider meaning or what was the fucking point? You nestled into him to keep warm and he wrapped you close to his body underneath his oversized coat. He smelled of sweat and weed. I'll keep you safe, he said. You believed him because right then you couldn't bear not to.

16

QUEER DEATH DRIVE

Your insides hurt, somehow. Somehow your insides have gotten hurt. Is that possible? *It is.* I haven't talked to you in a while. *Well, you're talking to me now.* Yes. My tummy hurts. *It does, I know that.* It's like ... cramped. Very painful. I'm in extreme discomfort. *Not just that.* No. *Your anus hurts.* Yeah. It stings. *And your head hurts.* I know. *You ache.* What happened? *How should I know?* I thought you were ... the sort of voice that knew things. *I know some things, I don't know others.* Do I have a hard on? *Yes.* Why? *You need to stop asking me that.* You said you knew some things. *I don't know anything you've asked me to tell you.* I want to throw up. *There's nothing inside you to throw up.* Did I shit myself? *Sort of. You made it to the toilet.* I remember now. *They're not inside you anymore.* Are you sure? *You got them all out. Or they were never in there to start with. You just had a very embarrassing drug hallucination.* Good one.

That's what happened. I can feel hands on me. *Breathe.* They put them inside of me, didn't they? *Just breathe.* They hurt me. *It'll be okay.* I want to die. *No you don't.* I want to die I want to die. *No you don't.* Get off me. *I'm not touching you.* Get off me! *I don't have hands.* Get off me!

~

"Get the fuck off me!"

The steaming water was too hot. It hurt. Everything hurt, and she could barely see.

"No ... no, it's okay." She knew that voice. It filled her with sickness, with rage, it made her want to vomit again, it made her want to scream.

Frankie tried to stand, but the bath she was in was slick and wet. As soon as she got halfway to her feet, over she went again. More pain. Their hands reached out to comfort her, but their touch stung.

"I'm trying to help," Vanya said, softly over the sound of the shower. "You're a mess."

"I'm fine." She was properly conscious now.

"We had to kick down the fucking door, Frankie. You'd gotten shit everywhere and passed out."

"I..." *I'd have been fine?* Was that what she really believed? Talking hurt. It took a colossal amount of effort. So, she gave up and just lay there in the bath. Vanya washed the faecal matter and the dried vomit from her body, like a wetnurse cleaning a helpless baby.

It was all wrong. The walls knew it. The dead bugs inside the ceiling lights knew it. Vanya knew it too. Something had been broken, and these were the pieces of it. Frankie's lovely dress lay torn in one corner of the room. It hadn't fit, sure. But it had cost so much money. All the hours and minutes of work that had gone into earning that money were for nothing. All the labour that had been poured into the construction of it: the threads, the silk, the spinning and the sewing. All those hands roughed by years of needle pricks. All torn apart, soaked in vomit and shit.

The hallucinogen, if that's what it had been, was no longer in her system. She must have thrown it all up.

"I saw things coming out of you," she said.

They wouldn't meet her eye. "I guessed."

"Were they ... that wasn't real?"

"I don't have things oozing out of my pussy, no." Their hands rubbed her thighs, but they were not tender.

"I'm sorry."

"It's okay."

"I think Gaz drugged me."

"Sure."

"Thank you for cleaning me."

"You called me a retard, Frankie. That's not ... That's too far."

The water splashed over her. That was all there was.

"You made me do something that I didn't want to do, that triggered my dysphoria."

"Sure," Frankie shrugged. "Did I kill your family too?"

"Once you're clean, dry yourself off. I'll give you some clothes. But after that, I never want to see you again."

She was too exhausted to protest. "Sure," she repeated. Sure. They didn't even walk her out of the house. They left that for Gaz, who smirked as he guided her through the front door. If any energy had been left inside her body, she'd have punched him.

"Fat tranny," he whispered in her ear as he pushed her outside into the early morning sun. His breath smelled sweet, like the syrup he had made her drink.

~

The sun was low in the sky. Gulls crossed in front of it. People all around her were heading to work, walking their dogs, being normal, well-adjusted people. Adults. *I'm twenty-eight, they just turned nineteen. Obviously it wasn't going to work.* She went into a corner shop and bought a bottle of water, a packet of fags, and a Bic lighter. *You've fucked much older guys though ... yes but that wasn't love, was it?* The cigarette was too much; she only smoked half of it. *Well, people have made it work.* She wanted to crawl into her bed and lie there for an entire day. *People, yes, but not you. You're a baby. They're a baby too. Baby4baby. Stop fucking theyfabs, go back to the fucking fags. Get knocked up. Get hate-crimed and left for dead somewhere. The possibilities are endless.*

Her bed didn't feel as comfortable as she had hoped it would. She texted the girls and said it was probably over between Vanya and her, but they left her on read. No tears for that entire day, but when the night came, she ordered noodles from the bar down the street and, halfway through, she was curled up bawling.

17

CENTIPEDE HORROR

He said he dreamed that you would be bitten by an infected mosquito and contract this type of parasitic worm that would cause your legs to swell to the size of tree trunks making you unable to walk there was no cure for that you'd just have to live in bed all day waiting for him to return and fuck you & feed you before leaving again. Eventually he offered you a place in his house & you took it & your mother never looked for you but she forbade your name from being spoken in your house she hit your sister if she asked your sister wanted her hair cut short and you felt so guilty you hoped he would never look at her funny because she was approaching the age when he had first looked at you around the same age you had a dream that he your brother he held you down and fucked you in the dream it was vivid you remembered the waning moon outside. You even remembered the pattern of the sweat on his brutish face. The dream. The dream. But no thank fuck he moved away soon after you did quite suddenly when he hit eighteen he went to Poland and got married there sees your grandparents all the time but rarely calls home. You shouldn't say those things about him he's your brother he loves you you love him he has a girlfriend he has a wife now and a job in an office there in Kraków he said he wanted to return to his roots motherfucker you've never been to Poland before you have no material connection to it it was only an abstract to you. He only went back because he hated his neighbours & they hated him. There were no Muslims in Poland he said he wasn't right but who was counting? He raped you, you know that. It wasn't a dream he said it was you know that you just think of it as a dream sometimes. So many fags in this city. Nobody even calls them that here that's American so what no fags in Poland no fags no Muslims no trannies no groomers see no Russian communist scum. You weren't ruined by what he did to you you'd probably have ended up in exactly the same place if he hadn't done it but it did affect your outlook on life & your relationship to your body & to sex & to deny that would be to deny the truth. He moved away he couldn't hurt your little sister his ideas weren't even his own but really, are anybody's? He got them from some YouTuber who got them from a YouTuber who got them from a Twitch streamer from TikTok a blogger who got them from a YouTuber who got them from a blogger who got them from a paper a journalist a mass shooter a YouTuber a Twitch streamer a YouTuber a Twitch streamer from discord from /pol/ from government policy from Mum. He bought a camera and makes videos about Polish folk traditions. In the videos he sits in his truck talking straight to camera. No one ever fucking watches. No one cares what he has to say nobody watches he is screaming into empty space. He lost the fucking lottery. He's a pathetic loser, his wife hates him and he sucks at his job and making fires in the woods won't change any of that. The only thing that gets him hard is thinking about his little sister. You make me sick. Kill yourself already.

18

CLOWN WORLD

And that was it. Vanya never attempted any sort of contact ever again.

After a long time, Jade did reply to her update in the group chat, saying that she was sorry to hear it was over. If Frankie needed anything, all she had to do was ask. Frankie didn't want to ask for anything.

She invited a man from Grindr to her flat and realised only once he'd told her he was on his way that her flat was a mess and she looked like shit. She rushed a shower and kicked rubbish under her bed. There was a clean set of lingerie at the bottom of a drawer, and a robe that looked kind of alright draped over it. She didn't need to dress up more than that, given it was all coming off again. He messaged an update that he was ten minutes away. So, ten minutes to put on a face. But the face that looked back at her once she was done didn't look like the face of a beautiful woman, or a hot girl, or anything close to how she wanted it to look. It looked like a fucking clown. The clown in the mirror pouted comedically. Well, she was about to get cream-pied, she supposed it was appropriate. Being with Vanya had stifled this particular intrusive thought. But Vanya wasn't there now.

She lit some scented candles. No time to douche, so no fucking her arse. Would he even want to fuck her cunt? Sometimes these guys only wanted to fuck her ass. It was a whole thing; she guessed that they probably just imagined they were fucking some femme guy. It was harder to trick yourself into believing that if what you were fucking was a pussy. The clown in the mirror looked like it might cry at any moment. It was pathetic really. Cheer up, cheer up, no one likes a sad fucking clown, they bum people out.

The guy didn't say much when she opened her door, but that was fine. He didn't complain about how she looked. He could probably tell that she was a bit fucked up. He seemed intoxicated. He kept itching his face and his breathing was short and shallow but hey, she thought, don't ask, don't tell. When he took his dick out, she wasn't disappointed. At his climax she let him – encouraged, begged him to – cum in her pussy, and then, after he'd gone, having said probably twenty words in total, she lifted her legs up into the air like a fifties housewife trying to conceive. She could still feel the cum inside her. She didn't want it to drip out; it was precious. She clenched her legs shut and willed the cum to work. In actual fact, it just sat there at the dead end of her vaginal canal.

Cis girls didn't even know how good they had it. Any given hook-up could knock them up. She'd never know that feeling. They didn't know how good they had it.

~

"Geez," said Wolf. "Frankie don't take this the wrong way, but you look fucking rough."

"Got broken up with," she said.

"Do you want to talk about it?"

"Nope."

Wolf shrugged. "If you say so." She stubbed out her cigarette and went back inside. A minute later, Frankie followed. As horrible as this job was, it was something. It pummelled her brain into a daze. After a long day of staring at all those threats of rape, she had no interest in looking at Vanya's Instagram. Not that they posted much anyway.

An author had been stabbed while giving a talk. He was in critical condition. The images of him lying in his blood were everywhere. The video of the stabbing kept reproducing itself. Just as she banned one version of the video, four others appeared. She didn't care about the author, she'd never read his books, but the way the knife sunk into his chest was chilling anyway. It *sunk* in. It didn't jab violently. It happened slowly. In real life, everything happens slower. Nobody reacts like they should. Everybody just watches it happen, mouths open in awe. That was how it was in the video: the guy who had been interviewing him just sat there like a fucking idiot, gawping.

"This is just the start," said somebody else on Twitter. "This is what they want to do to Jennifer Caldwell. This is what they'll do to anybody who steps out of line ..."

~

On the bus home, Frankie sat at the back, away from everybody else. The bus driver wasn't doing the best job. Every corner he took was too sharp, every stop too sudden. Rain dribbled down the windows, churning in the gullies and the gutters. Thick rain, thick as spit, she thought. But when it was her turn to get off the bus, she found that she was mistaken: it was just normal rain, as cold and as grim as ever. She walked into her flat, dried herself off, made a Pot Noodle and settled in for a night spent much like her day: scrolling social media. The only real difference was that she put the TV on, without really registering which American sitcom was playing.

There was a lot happening on Twitter. Some supposedly left-wing journalist tweeted, *Here's my piece for Quillette on why I think condoms lead to an epidemic of sexual and romantic unfulfillment.* In the replies, people thanked her for her honesty. Other people asked her if she had ever heard of AIDS. Some people said, *Louisa, are you really so stupid to have never heard of AIDS.* She replied, finally, to one of those messages. *Obviously I know what AIDS is,* she wrote, *I'm talking about straight people using condoms.* A little while later Louisa said that the people telling her to kill herself deserve everything that's coming to them. As far as Frankie had seen, nobody had told her to kill herself, and Frankie was very attuned to people telling people to kill themselves because of her job. Supporters sent Louisa love anyway. She told her supporters that she *won't let them win*. At the same time, Jennifer Caldwell – mutuals with Louisa – retweeted a *Medium* article by some fucking detransitioner, some (ex-)guy who claimed that Stonewall *forced* her to take hormones. Someone looked through her old tweets. She definitely once presented herself online as a man. She also appeared to have a habit of making antisemitic jokes. After the jokes were made known, people asked Mrs Caldwell if she still agreed with her, but Caldwell didn't respond.

Her bedroom window was open. Rain came in, soaked the carpet just under it. She didn't notice, curled up on the sofa. The world shrunk until it was just her body and the phone screen, then it shrunk even further. Her eyes hurt. She sent a reply to Jennifer, telling her she made her feel sick, and instantly Frankie's notifications exploded, hundreds and hundreds of replies, quote tweets, and messages all calling her a receding hairline AGP troon groomer 41% but (*Wolf of Wall Street* meme) *we can get those numbers up! Those are rookie numbers* but Frankie couldn't look away. A man spammed Frankie's mentions with pictures of clowns. Cartoon clowns, photographs of clowns. Clowns from horror films and clowns from children's films. Clowns. Each image was accompanied by words. *CLOWN WORLD*, he said, in endless repetition. *CLOWN WORLD ... CLOWN WORLD ... CLOWN WORLD ...*

His profile was just that. Every tweet he sent, ever reply, was a picture of a clown paired with the same message. The further down his account she scrolled, the more entranced she was. *CLOWN WORLD*, he said.

"Clown world," she muttered under her breath.

CLOWN WORLD.

"Clown world."

CLOWN WORLD

CLOWN WORLD

CLOWN WORLD

CLOWN WORLD ...

Maybe it wasn't so wrong to want to tear this all down? To burn the fucking place? But there are desperate people here just like you, people who don't deserve the same shit you got. It's so hellish, isn't it? Fluid leaking from Frankie's phone screen puddled next to her head, except it wasn't from the screen, of course it wasn't. It must have been dripping down through the roof. #Rainwater filtered through the eaves of her building, drizzling through the attic ... and she just kept scrolling. Each thing she saw was worse than the last. *Groomer. CRT. They are in your schools. They are in your walls. My swimming finals spot was stolen by a biological male. Until we all refuse to compete nothing will change. Thanks for all the support retweets and follows I wont stop fighting. Video of two dogs playing. I am eager and willing to work with members of Congress to put an end to this politically correct 'woke' madness! To protect the integrity of women!* #WomenWontBackDownFromYou #WomenWontShutUp *our little white girls having spheres cut from their torsos, they are eating their wombs, they are eating their aborted fetuses – trans women are eating aborted female fetuses to ingest hormone [REAL][NOT CLICKBAIT]SOMEBODY DO SOMETHING.*

At some point, in the middle of scrolling, she fell asleep.

~

It wasn't the restful sort of sleep. Frankie didn't dream much, but when she did, the dreams were deep and vivid. In the dream, sat on a throne, resplendent in a red robe, golden jewellery draped over her. Her lips were crimson in colour. The white room. A cisgender woman lay on her back in front of her, punching her own stomach, hard and getting harder. The woman was dressed in a burlap sack, and her legs were splayed wide. She punched her swollen stomach. With every impact, she groaned with what may well have been ecstasy. But Frankie, looking down at her, didn't feel anything at all. There were other figures in the room, dressed in some strange ceremonial outfits that hid their faces. There were no windows in the wall, so she had no idea where she might be. No windows, just featureless walls. The walls here were different to the walls where she came from. The geography of this city made no sense. The cis woman on the floor screamed and now finally she couldn't bear it anymore: her cunt was gaping wide, and she jammed her hand, open, up there, her face all red and tears streaming down from her eyes. One of the figures leaned close to whisper into Frankie's ear: "You are doing this. This is what the modern world looks like because this is what you want it to look like." Is it?

"I don't want this," she said. But what was the use? The woman, with one fist, pulled something out from inside of her. Here it came now, flailing into the light. She held it up triumphantly. It wasn't a baby. It didn't look much like a human at all. It dripped blood. It didn't have eyes. It certainly didn't have a heartbeat. The white floor was drenched in the gore that flowed out of the woman, but she didn't seem to care.

She held her child out to Frankie.

There was a fringe belief, which had gained traction over the past few years, that the *trans lobby,* whoever they were, kept children as sex slaves in the basement of their London offices.

Frankie didn't want to take the child. It repulsed her.

"I don't want to have someone else's child," she said. "You're ... this isn't what I wanted. It's just a stupid fetish! Leave me alone!"

It's not a fetish, it's a belief system. It's like fucking tradcaths. It's not a fetish if they commit to it fully. This isn't a fetish. You really want it.

"Don't tell me what I want!" But everyone around her, everyone dressed in red and gold, was so expectant she take this abortion and eat it, because they heard about it on some forum. People marched the streets of this strange city. Above its byzantine, bent towers, the moon reached towards the sun with uncaring tendrils.

~

At midnight she woke. Her body felt lethargic, but her mind was completely alert. There was only one thing to do, only one thing she *could* do. She looked at Twitter some more.

Dear Jennifer, wrote somebody, *thank you for your fearless advocation on behalf of women and girls everywhere. I was wondering if you knew about the rumours that the Stonewall organisation keep children in their basement for the purpose of abuse?*

Next tweet in the thread: *Did you know that the place the name comes from, the Stonewall in New York, was a sordid sex bar where drag queens with faces painted like grotesque clowns frequently raped and exploited children, and the only reason that the police was raiding it was to stop child sex trafficking?*

I didn't know that because it isn't true someone (not Caldwell) replied. The original poster called them a rape apologist.

"I advocate for children everywhere," Jennifer said once. She set up a charity for kids in need, kids with cancer, kids with weak hearts and tumours and no legs and no tongues. The villains in her book series were a race known as the Dark Elves. She advocated for children everywhere.

Caldwell posted a picture of herself drinking with a group of other middle-aged women. All of them wore T-shirts that bore the slogan *BIOLOGY IS REALITY*. Underneath, Frankie wrote: *I hope someone drops a bomb on all of you.*

19

SCREW THE ROSES

You had a sister. You never really talked to her. She was way more girly than you, she cared about Barbies and things like that which never interested you. When it became clear she was going to be like that you relinquished all older sibling duties. You found her annoying, you thought her voice was high pitched. Do you know how cruel that was? She was alone, all she had was your Mum. And you were wrong, anyway. If you bothered to spend time with her, if you hadn't run away like a coward, you would probably have been the first person he told: he wasn't a girl. He was a boy. He still liked pink sure, but he wanted to be a boy. As it stood you were gone before he realised that for sure. The first person he told was your Mum. You can imagine how that went. She blamed it on your influence even though again you had barely any relationship with him, to her you were no longer a real person you had ceased to be real when you left and now you had been cast as the Enemy by her, the Foe. You represented sin so it was your fault. He'd already told his teachers apparently his friends all used the correct pronouns for him but you missed him see, you didn't even know he used another name and you'd only find out when you were older, when it was too late. Your mother resisted telling your older brother but of course eventually she did. She told him. He sent her some articles which she consumed hungrily it was like reading everything she'd been thinking the transgender craze seducing her daughters literally her daughters thank you son thank you for this he said hopefully we can save little Ana before (((they))) destroy his body for good. What he didn't say was that your little sister/brother like you before him was needed to continue the family line. You were by this point a lost cause the last time he raped you was the only time he ever came inside you he did it when he knew you were ovulating but whatever you did to your body when you shoved that shit inside yourself whatever had happened to your insides they were as he would say barren so you didn't carry his child you just lay there you could feel his semen inside you it hurt more than the shit & the infections had it burned you you wished you could bite his face off that was the last time so he knew you were a lost cause if you weren't you'd have carried his kid right he thought in his head but little Ana there was still hope for her as long as she didn't let them tear out her womb. The things he did say & the things he sent were enough to give your mother the context she needed to the thoughts she already had. It led her down a series of hyperlinks to more blogs, to Mumsnet *and* UnHerd, Spiked, The Atlantic, *Twitter,* Facebook *and more. Her mind was fertile ground for the worms which spawned there. Your mother she grew parasites of her own* she was the perfect breeding ground ripe like the soil of an orchard. At the same time as this Gaz gave you ringworm it spread across your skin red crusty wheels under your skin itchy red crusty wheels He spanked you if He caught you itching them, his housemates didn't know he was very skilled at keeping everything under the radar they just thought he had given a home to an underage person desperately in need which to be fair he had done they just didn't know about the other stuff he was careful to do it to you in places you wouldn't see he said you were fertile (you were infertile) he said you were the perfect breeding ground you giggled well you know how to charm don't you and he winked but you were starting to feel the pain pain beyond the itching pain beyond the good pain that is, difficult pain that stretched out that hurt inside your head his father visited never but sometimes they talked on the telephone you were a breeding ground but you weren't half as fertile a plot as your own mother's brain was, alive with the glory of the universal truth from the moment she read that Caldwell piece onwards there was only one way to go now the fact that the only way to go now was down the fact that she started to look at strange websites the fact that she started to develop plans the fact that if she thought of you at all she thought with hate the fact that the fact that the fact that the fact that the fact that from Stormfront to The Guardian, the rallying cry was being called: they are entering your spaces and converting your kids, and they must be stopped. The clowns. The world was overflowing with violent clowns. It was a fact. It was just the facts. It was the fact that her husband had surely noticed changes about her now maybe he probably thought she was a lesbian because well because of the fact that she went to all those women's meetings the ones with women of a certain age (her age) who often had shorter hair and mischievous grins, the fact that when he asked what she did at those meetings she just said they were about women talking, surely he knew though surely he had seen her blood boil or maybe her youngest had said how she was acting, the fact that it was all your fault now you were gone & not coming back not missed most of the time the fact that she knew he thought he was the better parent of the two of them because he used the correct pronouns for Ana because he indulged in her teenage fantasy perhaps she should become a lesbian just to spite him although she didn't really want to kiss a woman and wouldn't know what to do once she had gotten to that point anyway and the fact that she'd never liked men and the fact that she'd been a tomboy, the fact that she knew that her daughter was just a tomboy but someone had told her differently. The fact that you can make a bomb from things you either already have about the house or, if not, things you can easily acquire from your local B&Q.

They deserved it they'd told her kid she was transgender, had told her that you could escape being a girl well you little bitch everyone gets periods and nobody likes them but the fact is you suck it up, deal with it, go on living, the fact that the very idea that there was some sort of escape made her feel a deep pit in her stomach as she looked around her house and wondered both if this was it and if this had to be it, her daughter was spending more time outside and she knew that was normal but those friends, the ones with dyed hair, they seemed like bad news, bad news indeed, and her older daughter, Vanya, fucking crackwhore Vanya, probably dead in some warehouse somewhere, she felt awful for her but the fact was you couldn't help some people, could you? Back in Poland in the rare messages she got from her son he said they had gay-free zones and well she thought that seemed a little extreme but maybe well it was the fact that she didn't even know how to approach giving the talk and never had to any of her kids, the fact that she had no real understanding of sex beyond the basics, the fact that she didn't like sex and she hoped her kids didn't either – was that the door, she thought to herself, putting down the bowl and picking up her phone. It was a cool evening. There were craneflies hitting their stupid heads against the kitchen window. It had started so simply, with her daughter wanting to wear a tie to her brother's first wedding, wanting to wear a little suit. And then ... thinking about what those monsters would do to her, the fact that she had watched over and over again videos of real-life double mastectomies online just to see if she could take it and had studied the ways the skin was sliced open and the tissue pulled out, the fact that, after, nipples would be gone completely and the chest was spoiled with two scars that arced across either side, the fact that she knew they wanted to do that to her little girl, she'd never know the joy of breastfeeding or whatever, the fact that breastfeeding was not really a joy or fun at all, it ached and by the end she gave up but regardless she still should have to know the pain of it, you couldn't just veto out of womanhood because you didn't like the smell of it you little cunt the world is not a place you make the world is a place you are made by, the fact that her suffragette colour knitting patterns couldn't save her, couldn't save anything or anyone. She built it in the garage over five months. He never looked, he never cared.

Bet you didn't know any of this, did you? You didn't know your mother was the one to blow that GIC up. You didn't know Frankie had nearly been killed by her. You look like your mother, Frankie saw you from across the club & was entranced she didn't know why but you reminded her of a forgotten face your mother's face the face that had planted the bomb that nearly killed her that's the only reason she wanted to fuck you, if you didn't look like her Frankie would never even have noticed you she'd have walked right past you & probably gone and fucked some guy & told him to impregnate her & he'd have been like uuuuh sure babe uhhh but just because you looked like her you caught her eye. Or I guess you could say it was shared trauma you were both victims of the same woman's selfish abusive parenting.

On your seventeenth birthday you were given the gift of tapeworm eggs. You'd lived at Gaz's for a while now slipped through the cracks out of the system see your mother never bothered to file you missing she threatened to hurt your father if he tried to.

Gaz was gentle. He only infected you with something once every few months so as not to attract attention from the other people who lived in his house rent-free you'd have happily done it every week be given multiple parasites at once you'd have happily been a host and only a host but he kept making you earn your keep in the garden or in cooking or other chores he needed you mobile or whatever but yes he gave you the tapeworms on your seventeenth birthday. He even put them up your arse for you. Damn Vanya, *he said, while he shoved them up there.* You were born with a fucking dick in your brain, weren't you? Fucked in the head. *It went on like this for a year. For over a year.*

See everyone in your life stood on a stage. Decorate the stage however you wish, if you wish to. You lay on the bare concrete, facing the ceiling. A hole had opened up there, but through it you couldn't see the stars, just orange light pollution from the Amex Stadium a few miles away. A hole opens up there, in the sky and inside your head. Time is crushed between the then and the now. In the warehouse this day, there are countless men. It is unclear if they are there at once, perhaps they are there at separate times, existing in the same space at distinct temporalities. Nobody speaks for a very long time. Nobody is looking at each other. They are all looking at other things. Finally one of them stands up and walks in a circle and says –

SPEAKER 1. Active monsters.

Active monsters. There is something in each of their interiors, which fills them up. This means they are constantly in the presence of another. The kitchen bin is clouded with fruit flies. One of them sits in front of the kitchen bin. The kitchen bin smells sweet. The audience are allowed to approach the bin and bend over it and sniff it deeply, if only they can avoid inhaling a fruit fly. This is what living alone is like. But none of the SPEAKERS live alone, they live in loose groups, and they are argumentative and know where they come from. Can you hear somebody saying something backstage in the backstage toilets saying something, a little too loudly, like they know they can be heard? This person is not meant to be saying anything.

ACCIDENTAL SPEAKER. It's blocked with … grapes? Someone has shoved loads of grapes down it, and now it is blocked.

The SPEAKERS look up and murmur at the interruption.

SPEAKER 4. Grapes?

SPEAKER 1. Active monsters.

SPEAKER 20. Take care of that sweet lil—

SPEAKER 3. We suggest limiting the wearing of internal devices to a few hours at a time.

SPEAKER 16. It's good to be King.

SPEAKER 8. Grapes.

SPEAKER 9. Internal.

SPEAKER 21. Suction.

SPEAKER 12. The bombs began to fall but then they never popped. They never popped. The children came and poked them with sticks but they never popped.

Now you realise that there is a picnic basket in among everyone sitting and speaking and listening. Inside the picnic basket is (naturally) a bundle of grapes, as well as a house, and inside the house is a woman and a man, and the man is making the woman lie on hot coals naked. Stop looking. The grapes have avoided the fruit flies. The cupboards are all filled with tiny black bugs, which get into your bags of rice. Wash the rice, then put it in a saucepan with water and a small amount of vegetable oil. Stir the water, rice, and vegetable oil. Pour in a cup of salt. Turn the burner on. Put a lid on the saucepan and go to the other side of the room and idly play with yourself while looking directly at the sun. When the water begins to boil turn the burner down and wait for the rice to rise to the top of the water. Then pour the whole mixture into the bin. The fruit flies are disturbed. SPEAKER 4 grabs your ankle and your scream.

SPEAKER 4. Suction.

SPEAKER 1. I just don't know how to approach you.

SPEAKER 19. He pressed a heated poker into my thigh and wrote out a word on there but I've never been able to make out what he was trying to write.

SPEAKER 17. He was trying to write out his address you stupid bitch.

SPEAKER 5. If you didn't want it in writing then why say you wanted it in writing?

SPEAKER 11. What did you have to lose?

SPEAKER 14 stands up and begins walking in circles on stage.

SPEAKER 14. You see I genuinely think I'd let you do whatever you wanted to do to me. Whatever you wanted. You're that special to me right? You're that important.

SPEAKER 6. I didn't think it was possible for me to feel like that about anyone.

SPEAKER 19. But I can't be around you without wanting to hide.

SPEAKER 9. Does it have to be that complicated?

SPEAKER 8. I just want to see that in writing.

SPEAKER 74. Who let you decide things.

Fuck.

SPEAKER 7 – desires to lose themselves to the fantasy.

SUGGESTIONS FOR MEETING IN PERSON

1. never use your real name in adverts, on forums, when advertising for meat.
2. get references. talk to her mother about what you want to do to her. tell her mother it is going to be alright.
3. meet in public, in an art gallery for instance.
4. where a level of pain is pain once again.
5. active monsters.

Where a level of pain is pain again. Active monsters.

SPEAKER 21. Where a level of pain is pain once again.

BRAINWYRMS

SPEAKER 1. Active monsters.

The couple who lives inside the picnic basket have bought a condo.

SPEAKER 6. Bloodied mess, but make sure she knows what she is.

SPEAKER 18. Do you know what I am? Do you? Truly? I don't know what I am. I looked in the mirror today and I only saw a bloodied mess, I only saw a vacuum, and you are like the thing that fills that void, the void that I am, the empty space, I am the nothing and you are suddenly God,
I am the dead bird and you are the hand holding a second dead bird,
I am the cunt
and you are the active monster
I am the cunt
and you are the synthetic meat,
I am hollow. I am hollow. I am hollow. I am hollow.

SPEAKERS 15, 7, 2, 9, 18, and 4 begin to dance.

SPEAKER 6. And so what if we are bloodied rags.

The fruit flies look agitated. They begin to swarm. They think something is coming.

The couple in the picnic basket have accidentally run over a neighbour's pet cat in their brand-new car.

Suddenly, the stage begins to look really stupid. It's obviously fake, but it looks fake in a stupid way now.

> SPEAKER 12. And so what if we are bloodied rags. And so what if I don't know your real name. I know your number I know your address, I have it here, that's enough right? Right? Right?

> SPEAKER 17. I literally live to serve.

> SPEAKER 3. Right?

> ACCIDENTAL SPEAKER. I can't see anything, can someone please let me see something?

> SPEAKER 7. Has it happened yet?

> SPEAKER 8. You're a genius and I love you so much.

SPEAKER 6. Don't look at the notes on my phone too carefully please.

Lights up on the corner of the stage, which is now a wooded area – rural intruding into urban. There is a rotting corpse on the ground, and SPEAKER 2 (I think?) is standing over it when they look up and meet SPEAKER 13's gaze. Their eye contact lasts only a second.

SPEAKER 9. Screw the roses. Send me the thorns. Screw the roses. Send me the aphids.

SPEAKER 21 grabs SPEAKER 15 and wraps barbed wire around its ankles. Or are they rose thorns? No, it's barbed wire. SPEAKER 9 calls the cops.

SPEAKER 15 tries to crawl and the rose thorns cut into his ankles and he begins to bleed. He starts to cry.

SPEAKER 15. Mummy. Mummy. Mummy. Mummy. Mummy. Mummy.

SPEAKER 21 pulls out a knife and cuts his phone number and address into SPEAKER 15's back.

All of the other SPEAKERS begin to echo
SPEAKER 15.

ALL SPEAKERS (apart from 21).
Mummy.   Mummy.   Mummy.   Mummy.
Mummy.   Mummy.   Mummy.   Mummy.
Mummy.   Mummy.   Mummy.   Mummy.
Mummy.

              Mummy.

Mummy.

              Mummy.

Mummy.

              Mummy.

Mummy.

              Mummy.

Mummy. I want my
Mummy
Mummy.

              Mummy.

Mummy.

              Mummy.

Mummy. I want my

              Mummy. I want my

Mummy.

              Mummy.

Mummy. I want

              Mummy.

Mummy.

                              Mummy. I want my

Mummy.

                              Mummy.

Mummy. I miss my

                              Mummy. You are my

Mummy. I need my

                              Mummy. I want my

Mummy. I miss

                              Mummy.

The couple in the picnic basket never told their
neighbour about the cat.

Mummy. I killed my

                              Mummy. I raped my

Mummy. I fucked my

                              Mummy. I am my own

The cops arrive and break everything up.

Mummy.

                              Mummy. Abolish my

Mummy. Deconstruct your

                              Mummy. Infect your

                              Mummy.

                              She stinks so bad

                              Your Mummy stinks

                              all your friends can

> smell her
> they all talk about how
> much she stinks & they
> make fun of you
> you're the one with the
> stinky Mum
> It's not her fault, you say
> She's got a condition
> She's got a condition it
> makes her stink but
> they laugh at you.
> Mummy
> Mummy

One cop looks longer at the scene and begins to mutter to himself.

> COP 4. Mummy. Mummy.
> Mummy.

He catches himself and walks away.

I thought you were a true believer, *he said.*

A believer in what?

He shook his head. Maybe you'd come around to it in the end. He said you would, but you weren't sure what he was talking about. You weren't sure if you believed in anything at all.

I just want to try being independent for a bit, *you said.* I'm not going anywhere I just want to ... go out clubbing.

Get drunk. Stuff like that. Can I do that? Do I have your permission, Daddy? If I don't I feel like I'll go fucking insane.

~

Frankie's piss was the best thing you had ever tasted; it was a fountain of life, it was amniotic fluid, champagne and the tears of God. You were like ah, this is what I've been looking for all this time. This is what my life was missing, somebody like this that I can touch & who will touch me & who will let me drink their piss & who is pretty & might buy me drinks. You were like oh shit am I falling in love at first sight though you had taken some mandy earlier in the evening so that probably affected things somewhat.

Gaz got grouchy. He texted all the time, too much. Frankie held onto one of your arms, Gaz held onto one of the others. Pulling until your body was like string. Frankie noticed that you gave him too much attention … She started to get suspicious of things, but she could never comprehend the truth. Frankie got rougher. How thin you were how dangerously thin compared to her she looked how a human should look she looked normal you looked like a ghost compared you sometimes thought you could see your insides through your skin.

Thank God Gaz didn't kick you out as you'd have had nowhere to live you did his chores for him you cooked for him he didn't ask to touch you now he just asked for stories of your tapeworm when the tick thing happened he got you to tell him about that too you admitted you knew that area was a hotspot for them he laughed good boy he said well, be careful. He didn't cut off his monthly payments either.

Then it happened, a little while into the relationship, you woke up feeling different. Luckily you weren't at Frankie's ... if this had happened at Frankie's you'd have been majorly fucked. The feeling intruded into your dream at first a wetness seeping in at the corners of the dream the wetness on the inside of your leg in the dream became the tongue of a great beast. You woke as the sun, freshly risen, pressed against your curtains & so you just lay there for a while enjoying the warmth the sun the dust motes that sort of thing before you became aware that the wetness was still there outside of the dream you thought you'd pissed the bed but you then saw what it really was you felt melancholic you felt relieved. For the first time in quite a while you logged back onto the old forum which you had stopped using when you moved into the house given that there was no real need to use it but you logged back in. Blackout curtains, it took a moment of lying there under the covers to work out what it was.

Last night *you said in your first post in years* I woke up to him curled around my legs tenderly like a lover. I felt him wet against my thighs. I thought that I had bled, or that I had shat myself, which I suppose I had, in a way. He had been inside my intestines for months, loving me, and then he had died and out he had come while I was asleep, a long, thin, wet thread entangled with my limbs. I yelped without meaning to and crawled away from him without meaning to. I had put a lamp on to see what had happened, and he glistened in the light. I had kicked him away and I felt guilty about that. He had just died. He had just died inside of me, and I had kicked him away in return, one last gutting rejection. Poor little guy. If I died inside of someone's intestinal tract I would want to be embraced, not kicked away in fright. But I have to confess that I did not embrace him or kiss his body, which was speckled with blood and with shit, I got up, left the room and slept in the bath. The next morning, I woke up and put him in a black bin liner, then I changed my sheets. *WebMD* says that tapeworms make you crave eating salt and dirt. They make you sick, and I've been sick, been in pain, but what was I going to do about it, who would I have told? Can I just go to the doctor and say doctor, I feel sick? I want to pour salt in my mouth and eat soil and my shit looks strange and my head hurts, and I know I have a tapeworm inside of me, I put it there myself. I didn't get the chance to love him back as he loved me. Don't be stupid I think, he didn't love me, he just wanted to eat the things that I ate, but he was inside of me, and I don't let things inside of me which I do not love, I know something's wrong with my head here. I lost a lot of weight, although that wasn't my reason for wanting to have one obviously. I loved having one inside of me, but over the last few months, when I had the tapeworm, my general health, both mental and physical, really took a nosedive. I was drugged up most of the time, but when I wasn't I was in severe pain, suffering from delusions. I saw all my friends around me like the players in a play. I literally thought my life was a stage play being acted out for me. Stuff like that. The tapeworm wasn't the only parasite I had, and I'm sure it wasn't great for him that I kept taking salvia, although he seemed to like it just as much as I did. But I stopped taking all those drugs. I stopped being so unhealthy. I met a girl, who I've been seeing for a while now. She has no idea what I'm into, and I'm not sure I'm ever going to tell her. And now he's gone, my tapeworm. He was expelled out of my little arsehole during the night, and I woke to him embracing me. When I was twelve, I was digging in the garden with a little spade and I found worms, I put them in a plastic bucket and I held them softly in my fist, I put them down my pants and felt them wriggling there against my prepubescent ... I knew it was shameful, disgusting, if Mum found out something awful would happen, I didn't even know why I was doing it but it was just the compulsion, see, to see what it would feel like, and guess what I felt it and it was bad, it felt good but the pit in my heart the confusion and guilt overwrote any pleasure I got out of it. The worms slipped out of my pants down my leg wriggling in panic and they fell onto the floor and I stepped on them all but the guilt didn't go away, it got worse. Now there were dead worms on the bottom of my sandals. And the sun was beating down. Mum was calling me inside, but she hadn't seen anything and I promised I would forget this ever happened.

My insides were, I guess, so toxic that they killed this tapeworm, and I have thrown him away so I can't think about him anymore, apart from that I wish I still had him.

I loved having something inside of me. Having someone inside of you is the closest form of intimacy, but with humans we can only experience this briefly during sex. With my worm he was inside of me all the time, for months on end. Where did I end and where did he start? I'm sad to see him go, but I don't plan on giving myself another one. It feels like a chapter has closed.

Love to you all,
Vee

You posted it despite the fact the forum was dead. You actually didn't realise that until after you posted it you just needed to get those words out of your system but then with curiosity you looked & saw yours was the first post to be put on the website in years now. Everybody had abandoned it. Half of the links no longer worked. You wondered if any of them were happy now, if they had forgotten their brief obsession and been assimilated smoothly into society in a way you knew you never could be. Surely that had happened to some of them, and the others? Well maybe this was yet another haunted house on the haunted internet. It was a dangerous thing what they did to themselves it had consequences it could go wrong.

Now we come to the truth of the matter, the whole stupid truth. I know you wouldn't admit it to yourself so there's no use waiting for you to say it: the simple fact was that it was never as good to actually do it as it was to dream about it. It was easy to write out erotic scenarios and discuss in detail what you wanted to do to someone. More than easy. It was brilliant. The most kinetic, beautiful thing in the world. But no matter how many times you carried something out in the real world – and the marks on your skin and insides showed just how many times that was – it was nothing compared to the fantasy. In the fantasy, having worms in your cunt or in your guts or in your head was utterly pure. In reality it was hot as fuck but it brought with it agonising pain, both physical and mental. The pain was obviously going to be part of it, it was even something that you found hot, but in reality it was still pain & discomfort. It wasn't just bruises or slaps or even slices, it was constant, and it got worse the more it went on. It was hot to walk around all day wearing a chastity device or a restrictive collar because, at the end of the day, those things could be removed easily. Their presence did not get more painful as time went on. People didn't make cock cages that tightened over a period of days. Perhaps they should. Perhaps this is all wrong, and that would be hot. Would you like it? Would you like to feel that?

I'm talking to YOU now ... not you, being Vanya. We'll get back to Vanya soon, I promise. I just want to address you for a moment because I think you've been ignored for far too long. You've gotten off easy, you deserve to feel the heat of the spotlight, so answer me this: would you like to have someone (not I) cage your cock up and throw away the key and then, over a period of time, over a period of days, weeks, months, or years, the cage ever so slowly would grow tighter and tighter. Maybe with every erection you have. Maybe unconnected to erections completely. I'm unsure which you'd prefer. No way out. No escape. Four months in and you can barely piss because your urethra is so restricted. It comes out like ... a dribble. It's to stop little slags like you from doing anything. It's to stop disgusting men like you from going out and hurting people. It's a castration. It's a way of life. It hurts. Five months in, and you notice it start to bleed. You stagger into work, and you stagger home again. You are never not in pain. It sounds good to you? Do you really think you'd like to be in such constant agony? Do you know you'd like that? I mean, would you actually like that or are you just telling me that to impress me? My Mum is listening to this. She didn't consent to hearing about your sick desires. I think it's actually disgusting that you'd go about in public like that. You get on the tube and go to work and go for lunch and go back to work and get on the tube and go home again, seeing hundreds of people every single day because you live in a big city. Not a single one of those people consented to being part of your game. Without anyone consenting, we've been drafted into it. There are kids around, you know, and there are traumatised women. Oh, but you say, isn't society one big game. What's the difference between this and seeing some men dressed up as adult babies out on a stag do? Well, that's the thing my dear. There's no difference at all. They're both wrong. Can't fucking outgame me bitch. I'm the winner, I'm fucking elite. I'll cancel my Dad without a second's thought. Look at him, the King there, dressed up in gold and silver and rubies and emeralds, being led down the strand on his golden horse. See the statue of Churchill. See the war memorial. The Marble Arch. Notice how the King doesn't walk anywhere? See, he misses his Mummy, and he's trying to do a good job to impress her. Under all that finery he's just like you. His cock's caged too. He's actually further along than you. You're a pussy, only five months in. He's been caged for two years, and he has to drain his bladder using a separate pipe that goes through his belly button. I'm not sure what he has down there could even be called a cock anymore, given how restricted it has become. But the thing he'd want you to know is that, after the first year, you sort of lose all feeling. It gets easier. But obviously, everyone was watching the coronation, and everyone, quite innocent, waving their little Union Jacks, cheering for the Royal Guard and the Beefeaters and the men and women in uniform, not a single one of them consented. I didn't consent to being part of this charade. There's no way out, though. They like to tell you if you don't like this country, you should just leave, but where am I going to go? Canada? New Zealand? Iceland? I can't go to NZ 'cause I'm too autistic. I'd be a burden on their health service, apparently. So, I guess I think you're sick, but I can't blame you given what this country's like. I'd be sick too if I had to be a man all day long. I'd want my cock destroyed too, if I had one.

Vanya. Vanya this is your internal monologue calling. Are you listening to me, or are you dreaming of having a cock again?

BRAINWYRMS

I wish I had a cock *you typed out in a message on your phone addressed to Frankie* I wish I had a cock just so I could know what it feels like to get your balls busted. *Backspace. Instead, you just wrote asking when Frankie was free next, a message which carried exactly the same feeling behind it. Maybe if you told Frankie then you could finally access that feeling you had been chasing but had never gotten, or at least Frankie, someone not part of the lifestyle, could still say to you hey, it's okay babe, it's unusual but you aren't sick for wanting that. God it didn't even fucking matter if she didn't want to do it, not really, you just wanted someone to listen and Frankie felt good it felt good when she listened to you when you folded into her body when you heard her heartbeat & she listened to you. You were really gonna tell her that night, when it was your birthday. You were gonna tell her! You had to tell her because however much you fucked, however good the fucking, you had over the last week started to think a lot more about the possibilities of fucking, see, you knew you were still so early in the relationship but you were getting horny again were you in trouble again the fucking was good the anal the fisting the piss all of that was good but you wanted to have your head locked in a glass cage, your mouth stretched open. You wanted to be force-fed, to have whiskey poured down your throat. You wanted to be unable to blink.* Frankie, fuck me, *you said when you were together, but it wasn't what you meant see you meant* Frankie, rape me. Frankie, mutilate me. Frankie, infect me. Fucking isn't enough anymore. I need you to kill me.

I can tell something's up *said Gaz.* Nothing's up. I know you *he said* I can tell when something is up. Frankie not hardcore enough for you? *You told him to shut up.* I've got such things to show to you Vanya. Such amazing things.

You really didn't know how to read what he was saying. If it's kids, kill yourself. Gaz laughed, it's not fucking kids. It's not fucking fucking kids I'm not a sicko.

Well why won't you tell me what it is?

I'd rather show you.

Gaz, I'm in a committed relationship.

Are you sure of that, have you talked about that?

Yes. I do what she says.

Doesn't sound too far from what we used to do. Just come and see.

Not if you won't tell me what it is.

It's just not something you can put into words.

It's life affirming.

It's life affirming?

You tried hard as you could to live in both worlds at once, even as it became clearer that it was impossible neither world fitted together but neither world made you feel whole how had some people worked it out made kink a natural part of their lives that was the dream was it to assimilate kink into capitalism along with everything else that was once subversive the forces were pushing up against each other true peak capitalism wanted everything it wanted the queers it wanted to market vodka to trans girls it wanted fetish weekend breaks but it had been brought about through alliance with a resurgence of right-wing religious Christian zealotry & these two forces once aligned somewhat were now starting to rub against one another creating painful friction because those zealots hated the degenerates but those capitalists were like the degenerates are a valuable market share you didn't want to be part of that & anyway the fetishes that were successfully or semi-successfully for now embraced by capitalism in the brief time before the neo-reactionary uprisings well those fetishes weren't even close to the things you liked you didn't care much for rubber or cock rings you wanted your womb to be used as a lab it was a little different you were a little harder to market to perhaps that was what Gaz meant when he said it wasn't just about the sex for him perhaps he saw his fetishes as inherently incompatible with the modern world yes that was it but whatever it was he was building whatever it was he wanted her to see it was something else something new beyond what you knew & that scared you you didn't know what he was capable of with all his money his resources his connections & ideas perhaps you were in too deep you thought perhaps you weren't as important as you thought in cosmic horror the fear is of an unknown far larger than you far greater a God that does not care for you may crush you as an afterthought we are all now experiencing the reality of this fear every day this is what we experience when we look at the internet when we look at Amazon Jeff Bezos may as well be a horned God because his distance from us is so astronomical he is woven into the fabric of our lives we cannot imagine life without Him yet to him we are nothing here this distance the fear of looking into the vast nothingness the fear that something might notice you you are constantly scared that the actions you carry out may be noticed that you are being surveilled you perform for the Gods/ for capitalism/for the surveillance state /for nobody the human reaction to the loss of distinction btwn subject & object this makes you (second person you not Vanya you) freak the fuck out makes you vomit and cry and scream shit your pants this is what we are experiencing on a mass scale all of us this is what the brain-wyrms are doing to our brains we don't even realise your brother remember made his little videos he made them for nobody at all yet he danced in them in his own way his own ridiculous jester's dance trying to get the attention of something larger than himself some impossible-to-comprehend force not individual just a great mass the great mass of culture being right-wing online sometimes seems like such an easy grift getting cancelled seems like such an easy grift in many ways it can be only if you are the right kind of person your brother was not the right kind of person nobody watched him dance nobody watched his dance nobody apart from sometimes you. Did that make you God to him? Did that give you power over him? You found his videos and sometimes you watched them he had grown he sat in the front seat of his car and spoke in English with an accent rarely if ever looking at the camera. You wished you had the courage to comment under one of the videos it's me Vanya I am looking at you because you could imagine just how scared he might feel but you had no interest in exposing him it didn't even occur to you as a thing you could do you just watched him and you thought about what he had done for you you touched yourself you wished he'd shared your fetish you didn't actually wish that of course but you fantasised about how it would have been if he'd forced larvae into your mouth you didn't wish it happened you could just daydream about it. Which was nice.

You watched one of his videos right after you told Frankie to leave. Gaz told you to tell her to leave. He said finally it's over, see, she doesn't care about you she freaked out at you she saw worms in your cunt if she reacted like that she called you r word she said you disgusted her she made you do things you didn't want to, right? Did I ever make you do anything you didn't want to? No, Gaz. Everything I did for you I wanted to do. You realised he was right of course if she was so disgusted by her vision which uncannily echoed reality then she would not have been able to handle reality at all it would have broken her mind Gaz said you won't be able to keep up not telling her you will get desperate again I know you I know how you are. She hurt you. She did. Gaz wouldn't hurt you. Or, the hurt from Gaz was the hurt you knew. She made you stop texting him, she looked through your phone, she bruised your face, she made you dysphoric, you hated her, you spat upon her image.

I'll be gentle, *he said.*

What is it that you were so eager to show me? *You asked him.*

I'll show you soon, *he said,* don't worry at all I'll show you soon. I told them all about you. They're very keen to meet you.

Who are they?

You wouldn't even believe me, nobody would believe you if you told anyone.

His gentle introduction back into parasitic life was a botfly bite on your right shoulder blade which swelled with yellow pus over the next few days just like that one you had seen back on the now-dead forum you looked at it with wonder in the bathroom mirror you knew you shouldn't pop it but standing naked in your bathroom the impulse was irresistible. It was tough to bend your right arm back but you managed to, and with the index finger of your right hand and the index finger of your left hand reaching over your shoulder you squeezed. The flesh around the bite was bright red and inflamed. The moment you touched it your felt it sting so sharp your eyes watered. This is what you get. This is what you deserve. The mirror was filthy with smears and water stains. It was a little off-centre, so your face in the glass seemed to stretch unnaturally downwards on the left side. It made your mouth droop down and your eye appear enlarged. You squeezed again and the pain exploded & the yellow head of the spot popped like a firework through the air, over the glass. You wiped your tears away you'll never be more than this a weeping wound filled with pus a breeding ground a host to bacteria a thing without feeling you do not belong to you you belong to all the things that live in you & that was beautiful you wished you could just pop yourself entirely you missed Frankie so much you blocked her number you never saw her say she thought she might hurt herself that might have complicated your feelings a little you wished you could pop yourself open you wished you were piled gross on the bathroom floor Gaz came in and found you you'd disappeared for a while he picked you up he put you to bed you gave in you gave up.

You were okay. He was gentle with you. He kept making you wait, it wasn't the time yet for you to experience these things, wasn't the time at all. You sobbed and begged for his cock but he denied it for perhaps the first time ever he denied it he would only touch you to hug you softly. It wasn't time yet. It wasn't time *yet.* You know she treated you badly, *he said.* Frankie? Yes, *he said,* Frankie, she treated you like you were her plaything. But, *you said,* you treat me like that too ... *and he said,* yes, because you're *my* plaything, but you weren't ever hers. *He told you to block her on everything, which you did. He said you shouldn't think so much about her. And you tried your best to focus only on the present to not spiral you didn't self-harm for a week. But then it all came flooding back when you saw your mother on the new.*

20

FAMILY
ANNIHILATION

Xavier walked from the little kitchen into the social space, trying his hardest not to spill either of the drinks he carried. In one cup was strong tea, with the bag still in, for Chloe, and in the other black coffee with three heaped spoons of sugar stirred in for himself. He managed to only spill one of them, the coffee, and even then only a little bit. A hot droplet of coffee rolled down the side and onto his finger. It hurt but he didn't drop the cup.

"Thanks, babe," said Chloe, taking her tea from him. She had turned up to the group feeling self-conscious about the fact that she hadn't had time to shave her face that day. He told her he really couldn't see any facial hair and she thanked him for lying to be nice, but he wasn't lying. He genuinely couldn't. Her face looked as soft and smooth and hairless as his own.

He sat down on the chair next to her and gave her an awkward smile. His drink was too sweet. He drank it anyway. Others joined them with hot drinks of their own or with orange or lemon squash in thin plastic cups, the type that split the moment they were squeezed. Everyone sat in a loose circle on the mismatching chairs. The AC was on, it was just a tiny bit too loud. Matt walked into the room and took his place in the circle, and the meeting began.

Xavier had started coming to the youth group earlier that year, after his father told him about it. For a number of reasons, he had felt hesitant to go, but Dad had said he thought it would be good for him and had promised to help him keep the fact that it was an *LGBT* youth group on the down-low. He said, "I'm not sure what your Mum will think, so let's just keep it between us for now", and Xavier hugged him very tightly. As his Mum grew more difficult, he grew closer to his Dad. They did not entirely understand each other, and potentially they never would, but it was good to feel closer to him. His Dad was quiet and unassuming, a balding Polish man who spent most of his days on various building sites supervising rookies. He wasn't the sort of person Xavier would have expected to understand certain things, but he did his best. Xavier's Mum was different, difficult. She was angry all the time now, and she spent most of her time on her laptop. She shouted a lot, she was quick to anger, she had worms in her brain, that was how Xavier thought of her: she had worms all up in her brain and they were driving her mad. It was easier to think of it in those terms than to admit that his mother genuinely hated him. Right now, she thought he was at a youth painting group.

They went around the circle, stating what they wanted to be called, their pronouns, and one exciting thing they'd done or seen this week. Xavier was new enough to the group that he sometimes hesitated saying his own name. It didn't yet feel *natural* coming out of his mouth the way his deadname did, but one of the older members told him that was normal, and he'd feel comfortable saying it soon. He was just unlearning things, it took time. "I'm ... Xavier," he said, when his turn came. "He and him, and um ... my Dad said he might buy me a binder! That was exciting."

"Fuck yeah!" said Chloe.

Matt gave her an exaggerated cartoon frown. "No swearing, Chloe."

"Sorry," she said. She looked a little sheepish.

Kensi smiled at Xavier from across the circle. "That's so cool, though," he said. "If you need any advice man ... I got you."

"Thanks," said Xavier, looking down at his lap. He blushed. Everyone was looking at him. But then it was Chloe's turn to introduce herself, so attention shifted away from him. Chloe was so pretty. He wished she knew how pretty she was.

That day, he got home and found his Mum in a foul mood, but she didn't seem to have any knowledge as to the true nature of where he'd been, and for that he was very grateful. He just let her sit hunched up on the couch on her iPad, tapping away at some argument on the internet. She barely acknowledged him when he walked through the door, but his father was there too, and he gave him a cut nod, the sort of nod an emotionally cut-off man might give to his son. Yet another affirmation, albeit one so subtle he wasn't sure if he had just imagined it.

The family had fallen apart a few years ago. Xavier's older sister had run away from home, and his older brother had moved to Poland and got married. He hadn't seen either of them since they'd left, although sometimes his brother called his Mum and they had hurried, secretive video chats. Xavier's paranoia told him *they're talking about you*, but he couldn't be sure, they could have been talking about anything. The house they lived in was frigid, its walls were bare.

"Your mother ..." his father said to him that weekend. "I don't really know what to do."

"What do you mean?"

"She's just *obsessed* with this stuff. It's all she talks about. I'm sorry, I shouldn't be telling you any of this."

"No, it's fine." They could hear her moving about upstairs. Her footsteps were heavy and luckily her whereabouts were quite easy to track.

"Ana ... sorry, Xavier. I want to keep you safe, but I don't know how."

He hugged his Dad. "It's okay, Dad. I know you do." *Please just get me out of here, please just take me and run.* He was old enough to know it wasn't that simple, and couldn't ever be that simple, but he still dreamt that it could be. Vanya had run away, why not him? Vanya was a different case, his father would say. *I should have done better by her.* Xavier barely ever saw his mother's face now, but the times he did he found it difficult to recognise. Her skin looked looser than it had been before, and paler. Perhaps she never went outside.

~

The next time Xavier went to the group, Chloe asked if he wanted to walk home with her, seemingly out of nowhere. "You live in Leigh Park, right? I don't live too far away from there, so you won't be going out of your way ... I mean, if you want to, no pressure."

"Of course!" he said, perhaps a little too eagerly. "Yeah, I live that way. I didn't realise you did as well."

"It's better to walk back with someone," she said. "Makes them think we come in packs, makes them back off."

He couldn't help but feel a tiny bit disappointed if that was her sole reason for asking him to walk home, but he tried to focus on the positives. It was a little difficult that day because his Mum had screamed at him earlier. It was the first time she'd even spoken to him properly all week beyond just grunts. She'd glared at him over the screen of her tablet, and her eyes were bloodshot. It started off relatively innocuously: she'd asked him if he'd read those Jennifer Caldwell books she'd bought for him. He lied and told her he hadn't been in the mood for reading. She asked him why not, he said he just got distracted, she said he didn't have ADHD, he said he wasn't saying he did, and her voice started to rise in pitch until it was a guttural bellow calling him an ungrateful little brat. He was dreading arriving home that day, so if nothing else, it would be good to walk back with somebody before he had to deal with whatever wreckage awaited him. If he was lucky, his Mum might have tired herself out and gone to bed early, or shut herself away in the old office. If he was unlucky, she'd be out and about, prowling around the house like an apex predator.

After the meeting Xavier and Chloe set off on their walk home. It wasn't particularly scenic as routes went – down North Road and then through Fratton – but he walked it so often he barely thought about it, unless somebody said something to him, or looked at him for just a second too long. It felt so much better with Chloe there. There were crows hanging out in the trees that burst from the pavement, and they suddenly seemed like such miraculous things when she was the one pointing them out.

"Don't you just think it's so cool," she said, "that we live in a city that's filled with nature like that?"

"I guess so," he laughed. She smiled at him, and his heart did a sort of twirl inside his chest. "I've never looked at it that way."

"There's foxes near where I live. They don't even realise that the city *is* the city! They just think it's all natural, they just think we're all animals. Maybe we are."

He didn't believe her; he didn't disbelieve her either though. He just thought she looked lovely when she talked like this, and he felt very grateful they had this time together. When they arrived outside her house, he asked if she wanted to go for a coffee in town sometime. She hugged him and said yes. She kissed him on his right cheek and disappeared up the stairs towards her flat. He watched her go, some tears in his eyes, before turning away and heading in the direction of his own house. He was still smiling when he got to the front door. His Mum was the furthest thing from his mind. But when his key turned, he could immediately sense something was wrong. He could *smell* it. There was a coppery odour hanging in the hallway, and the house was very quiet.

"Dad?" he called. "Mum?" He shut the door behind him. The lock clicked. At the end of the hallway was a dark stain on the carpet, right outside the open living room door. He was sure it hadn't been there before. He walked towards it. It looked like a wine stain. Near the large spot of the stain there were smaller droplets that led through into the living room, as if somebody had upended a red wine bottle and then walked with it still dripping through the doorway. He followed the trail. In the living room the light was low. Dad lay on the carpet. Vanya used to lie in that exact spot, watching TV for hours on end, but she had lain on her front, stretched out, relaxed like a large cat. Dad lay crumpled on his side, his head turned away from the lifeless television screen. His eyes were open.

"Dad?" Xavier ran to crouch at his side, but he didn't move. Behind him, right next to his head, was a metal rolling pin. He rolled him over and saw that one whole side of his head had been crumpled in by the rolling pin, shattered so much that the eye had disappeared under a torrent of blood. He was heavy and motionless and a corpse.

Fuck. This had never occurred to Xavier as a possibility. It felt so surreal that he was half convinced it was a nightmare, or a fantasy of some kind, and he was still wondering if that was the case when he heard her footsteps outside the room in the hallway. *Thump, thump, thump.* He turned. None of the lights were on in the house, and the sun was setting outside. She stood in shadow in the doorway, like a spectre. Nothing like his Mum at all, not remotely anything like his Mum, even if she looked like her, spoke like her, dressed like her, even though she *was* her.

"Ana," she said. "Where have you been?"

He tried to smile. "I was just at my youth group, Mum. You know that."

"What kind of youth group was it?" She was so still, and so thin ... he could probably squeeze right past her if it came to it. And surely she couldn't be that strong, could she?

"Just a normal youth group," he said. "We just meet up and ... hang out." It was stupid lying to her. She knew already, somehow. Maybe she had beaten it out of his Dad with the rolling pin. He hoped he had resisted for as long as he could.

"Don't you even think about going for your fucking phone you little bitch," said his Mum. "I'm going to give you one more chance to be honest with me. What kind of fucking youth group was it?"

He lifted one hand and wiped tears from his eyes. The hand was shaking uncontrollably. "It was an LGBT youth group," he said.

"Was that so hard?"

"No ... No, it wasn't ..." He bit into his lip so hard that it drew blood. His Mum moved through the doorway, out of the shadow that had been cast across her face. Now he could see her properly, even if the light was still dim. *Oh God*, he thought. *Her eyes.* "Mummy ... what's happened to your eyes?"

The knife in her hand flashed as it caught the last of the setting sun through the window. "I have seen it, Ana. I've seen it all. I've seen a terrible fate for this country."

"Mummy, please just stop this, please." His breathing was all shallow, which he knew was bad. He knew that meant he wasn't getting enough oxygen. But there were *things* dangling from his mother's eyes, writhing things. The skin of her face hung slack from her bones.

"We live in a world of clueless clowns." She raised the knife high up in the air. "You think you can just *opt out* of womanhood? You really think that's a possibility? You're a coward, Ana, and I will not have raised a coward."

He tried his best to be brave. "Your other son ran away to Poland."

She *hissed* at him. "I only have one son, you ungrateful little brat. You're just like your whore sister. You dream of some impossible world. Well, I've seen the future and let me tell you now: the world you dream of, it doesn't come true. It never does."

She lunged forwards into the room, the knife out in front of her. He surprised himself by how swiftly he moved, ducking right under the arm that held the blade and towards the door. He should have grabbed the fucking rolling pin, though. She stumbled and failed to grab him, and now he was out in the corridor. The front door was close, he could make it. On the wall in front of him hung a picture of his parents on their wedding day. He grabbed it and threw it at her as she wheeled about behind him. It connected with her; the glass shattered. *Yes!* He kept going, desperate to get to the end of the corridor. The door was in sight, the door was within reach. He could hear his mother's footsteps behind him, but she was only just out of the living room. He was going to make it out the door... but when he got there it didn't open. It had locked automatically when he came in. The handle just stayed still as he pulled on it pathetically. Those heavy footsteps were getting closer. He wasn't going to turn around; he wasn't going to give her that. There was a tiny switch next to the doorhandle that had to be pressed down to open the door. Fucking stupid not remembering that. Lost valuable time. But it clicked and he got the door open. The sun outside was nearly down and some of the streetlights were coming to life. He didn't bother opening the door wide, he just shoved himself, left arm first, through the opening, but now her hands were on him, pulling him back into the house. He felt her body pressing into his, and one of her hands pulling him back by the throat. His arm was still reaching through the open gap, but she kicked the door shut on his arm. The bone inside shattered. He screamed, and she dragged him back into the hallway. He tried to wriggle out of her grip, but she was far, far too strong.

"Mummy," he said between sobs. "Please Mummy, please don't."

She threw him onto the floor and crouched over him like a gargoyle with the knife against his throat. "I blew up a fucking clinic to stop them from taking you," she said, "I shouldn't have done that. I should have known it was all down to you. You were too far gone."

"Please Mummy, I'm ... I'm your baby. I'm your baby."

"Yes, you are," she said. The tip of her knife stroked his cheek. "You're my little baby girl. You'll always be my little baby girl."

Up into the air went the knife, and then it came down, down, and down again, until his insides were open to the breeze that gently rolled in through the open door. When the cops came, they couldn't believe how much blood there was. They'd never seen this much blood before: blood all the way up the walls, blood soaked into the carpet, blood on the shoe rack, on the landline telephone by the front door, blood on the flowers and blood in the vase the flowers sat in. Dad, Mum and kid, all dead. They couldn't understand why she'd done it, or even what it was she had done. It looked like she'd tried to cut open her own face, like she was trying to get something out from the inside of her head.

PART THREE

BRAINWORMS

Lovecraft understood the epistemological affinity between natural science and programmatic (as opposed to doctrinal) occultism, since both venture into regions once declared mysterious, following procedures of a rigorously calculative-problematical type. It is the alliance between purely speculative metaphysics and common sense that betrays such affairs of pure reason to futility, since they lack the calculative traction to revise their own conventional notions on the basis of their encounters. Practices – however implausible their guiding motivations – can know nothing of absolute mystery or metaphysical transcendence because their realm of certainty is procedural-problematic and uncontroversial, whereas their reserve of knowledge is empirical, refutable, repeatable, revisable, nonmystical and accumulable.

Nick L@nd, 'Qabbala 101', *Fanged Noumena: Collected Writings 1987–2007*

1

VISIBILITY POLITICS

"Look at me," she said.

"Frankie ... I don't want to do this. You know that, don't you?" But he still didn't look. He couldn't.

"Look me in the eyes if you're going to fire me."

He kept going, regardless. His eyes were firmly fixed on his desktop computer screen, as if he was firing that rather than her.

It wasn't a surprise. Ever since she had woken up the morning after sending that tweet, it had been obvious there would be some sort of professional repercussion. *I hope someone drops a bomb on all of you.* Not her most dignified moment, and not the best choice of words for someone known to have actually survived a bomb.

There were many possible defences she could mount – that she thought it was a dream, that it was perfectly justified to say extreme things back to people, but *The Times* had run a story on it, the headline reading 'Bombing survivor's sick tweets to Jennifer Caldwell'. That story probably sealed the deal. They wanted blood.

Bleary-eyed, she looked at her phone right after she'd woken. It showed a lot of notifications, but when she tried to look at them there was nothing at all. Her Twitter account was dead; nothing was left. Somebody with a job very much like her own had banned it. When she saw her emails, she knew this was bigger than just Twitter. There were requests for comment from journalists, messages from people she hadn't spoken to in years. Lula and Jade both messaged in the group chat, asking if they could see her. Then her phone started ringing. Ring, ring, ring. No matter how many calls she rejected. No matter if she put it on silent. If she turned it off, she swore she could still feel it buzzing, so she threw it against the wall. When she crept, like a frightened animal, towards it, she saw it laying on the ground, face up. Its screen was spiderwebbed with cracks. Those cracks seemed to widen as she stared at them, spreading further, outward from the phone. Everything was cracking, the fluid leaking through, diluting reality and poisoning it.

And then the next time she went into work, Kevin called her in for a meeting, and he spent that entire meeting staring at his computer screen.

"Look," she said. "I've been having a bad time. It was a lapse in judgement."

"I know. It's more a PR thing, you know. It's not anything personal."

"Just say I'm doing training ..."

He sighed. "It's not that simple, Frankie. It's not ..." He turned, his eyes gliding right past her, so he was looking at the wall just above her head. "I'm very sorry. You know I am."

"I need this fucking job, Kevin. I won't get another job easily, not after this. Cut me some slack, please."

On his desk, there was a little potted cactus. She thought about picking it up and throwing it at him.

"I'll suck your dick," she said. "If you want, I'll suck your dick, if that'll get you to change your mind."

Now he looked at her. "Fucking hell, Frankie. Get out of my office. Get out of the building. The ... I'll get security to help you out. We'll send you your P45."

Wolf waited for her in the hallway. "Them's the breaks," she said. Frankie walked right past her.

Seven months later, Wolf will jump from a bridge over a motorway. She won't leave a note, but a private Twitter account belonging to her will post a series of distressing tweets claiming that she is being sent coded messages through the posts she sees at work, and that the messages are telling her to, quote unquote, *do something drastic*. Frankie will never hear about any of this. *I have to do something & idk if ... I can. I'm scared im fucked in the head.* This will be Wolf's last tweet. The closest thing she'll leave to a will.

The whole ride home on the bus, the walk from the bus to the shop to buy rum and a packet of fags, the time in the shop, and the short walk from the shop to her flat: nobody met Frankie's eye. Not one person. *Do they know? Do they know you told beloved children's author Jennifer Caldwell that she should be bombed? Do they know you were the one who stumbled out of that GIC? Do they know you're a cumslut?*

"Fucking look at me!" she screamed at the man walking past her, right outside her building. And he did. He looked right at her, and he looked scared. Then he hurried on his way.

2

CRACKING
APART

What was that fucking Leonard Cohen line again? "There are cracks in everything ... that's how the light gets in"? Well, that wasn't realistic. When there are cracks in everything, it suggests a fundamental fragility. At every moment, Frankie wondered if her phone was going to shatter completely. When she used it, as she was using it now, the tips of her fingers tingled with a thousand tiny shocks. *im fine,* she typed. *like really im fine. just a rough week.* The cracks on her phone were evidence of the week's roughness. Her legs hurt. There were thin cuts on both her thighs, not deep but long, all the way down to the backs of her knees. It cleared her mind in the moment, but the aftermath was punishment for desiring clarity. Walking hurt now, just because she wanted to drown out the noise for a measly minute.

Sometimes, it was nice to push a sewing needle under a couple of layers of skin and keep it there. That stretched out the clarity longer than a minute. Sooner or later though, the needle had to be removed, and then, again, the damage had to be endured. If she was lucky, just a spot of blood. If she was unlucky, she would have nicked an artery. These were the cracks in herself. New ones appeared as fast as her body could heal them. She knew her limits and never crossed them. Well, almost never. One night, when she was quite drunk, she texted a picture of the cuts on her right thigh to Vanya's number. She knew it went through because she saw the read receipt, she saw those two little ticks flash up next to the picture. Vanya didn't reply, but knowing they'd seen it was as powerful an intoxicant as anything she'd drunk. The following morning, she felt like shit about it though. That *was* too far. Way over the line. *I'm sorry about that,* she texted, or tried to. The message bounced back. Her number had been blocked.

The Absolut vodka billboard was burned down. The smell of the smoke pulled her out of her sleep. It hung underneath her ceiling, more blowing in all the time through the open window. First, of course, she panicked. Her animal brain recognised the smell and knew what it meant. Her fucking flat was burning, she was going to burn to death, burn alive. But then, when she sat up, she saw the fire outside on the street below her window, billowing out black smoke. The flames licked the trans girl model's face until the paper she was printed on curled and distorted. And around the burning billboard were six figures with hoods pulled up, ski masks obscuring their faces. She heard one of them shout, the voice of a middle-aged woman, but what she said was obscured by the roaring of the flames and the sound of a fire engine approaching. The crowd dispersed.

The billboard had just been stupid corporate Pride bullshit. But even that wasn't safe now, she supposed. She had hated it, hated its cloying tone, hated the way it made her feel lonely. But now it was gone and there was nothing left. She tried not to think about this sort of thing too much, but looking down at the fire she realised that things were going to get very, very bad, and that she should probably get out of this country before it was too late, or consider detransitioning, or just kill herself. Things were getting very bad very fast.

She saw a news story about a young *trans-identifying* child who had been killed by his mother. The newsreader hated calling him a boy, she could tell. She could see the way her lip curled into a snarl as she said it. The mother had killed the boy's father too, and then herself. Family annihilation. That's what it was called. Nobody left alive to tell the story of how or why. Only journalists hastily reconstructing the facts of the case into a believable narrative, potentially close to the truth but never actually true. Frankie *had* lived, so she had been able to tell her story, even if some people never believed it. More people than before, since the whole Caldwell tweet. Lots of people thought there was something wrong with her.

Her train of thought was halted, brutally, when they showed the mother's face. The same face she'd never been able to recall in her waking life. A completely unremarkable face in many aspects, but one that had imprinted itself into her soul. She sank to the floor, staring with stupefied eyes. *Fuck.* The woman on the TV, shown in the picture hugging her two children. She looked so much like her eldest. The television might as well have been cracking, too, for all she knew. Even when the story changed to something else, some migrant crisis, she still saw that picture and she choked on air thinking about it. The woman who'd bombed the fucking clinic was Vanya's mother. The only reason she'd been so fucking obsessed with Vanya was because they reminded her of their mother. That was the only reason. They weren't special at all. They weren't even particularly beautiful. They just looked a lot like that fucking cunt bitch who now had murdered the rest of Vanya's family.

Sometimes, the world is so pointless and cruel, that the only logical, sane response is to tear out one's eyes. Frankie wanted to, and she even tried, before giving up and lying, spasming with sobs, on her carpet.

You stupid fucking slut, she kept saying to herself. *What have you done? What have you done?*

3

DRUNK
SLUT

Frankie was drunk enough that making the journey to Vanya's front door didn't seem like a terrible idea. It might not have seemed a terrible idea sober, either; she no longer knew where her own limits were. Nobody had bothered to deal with the burned billboard. It had been torched days ago, all the paper was scorched black. Two-hundred and forty inches of smiling feminine solidarity and love transformed into flaking charcoal. Even this country's cunty faux-liberalism would soon be dead, along with her, probably. *Along with everything else.* As she walked, she swigged from the bottle of Echo Falls she'd gotten from the corner shop. Sometimes the acid reflux in her throat was too much and her head hurt, so she spat aubergine-coloured wine onto the pavement between her feet.

The people she walked past kept looking at her. Thank fuck. They weren't pretending she didn't exist, they were *looking* at her. *Fat tranny.* When the bottle was empty, she left it in a communal bin and kept walking. It was too busy out there. Everybody was going out somewhere, or migrating between bars: groups of gay men, shit makeup smeared over their faces, scuttling together like one many-legged organism, clicking and cooing. Straight girls with makeup even worse than that of the gay men, squeezed into dresses two sizes too small. *They still look better than me,* she thought. She glared at one group, and made eye contact with one of the girls, her dyed-blonde hair framing the fake tan of her face perfectly. The girl recoiled. She wouldn't have helped Frankie in distress, obviously. She wouldn't have descended like an angel from on high. She'd leave her in the muck.

By the time Frankie was in Vanya's neighbourhood her legs ached and all she wanted to do was lie down somewhere. The streetlights pulsated and bent like reeds in a sea breeze. The moon in the sky dripped its yellow light down the inky dark. Everything was discoloured, like an oil painting left in the rain. She'd been expecting to find the crescent they lived on deserted beyond lights in the windows, but the moment she turned onto it she sensed that something was strange. There were people there, further along the row of houses. They stood outside, milling around in a large group beneath a streetlight. It was difficult for Frankie to see properly, but she knew, obviously, that she shouldn't just approach the group openly. Even in her addled state, she was in possession of enough brain cells to avoid doing that. Instead, she crossed to the other side of the street and moved slowly, keeping her distance.

Was it her drunkenness, or was everybody in the crowd dressed the same? As she skulked closer, she was sure they were all wearing hooded black cloaks that obscured their faces and forms. There were maybe twenty people, but as she hid in the shadows between a car and a tree, another car rolled down the street and stopped, and two more figures dressed in the same garb got out. The others turned and nodded at them. Frankie had been so entranced by the strange outfits that she hadn't realised the most jarring fact: the group wasn't just lingering on Vanya's street ... it was standing right outside their house.

Why the fuck had she even come there? What was the plan? She'd been thinking she might stand on Vanya's front step and call up to their bedroom like a hopeless romantic. As if that would have won them back. As if anything could. But this was much more interesting, she thought. Maybe it was a theme party, or an orgy. Maybe Gaz was a freemason or something of the sort.

As she watched, the front door opened. Another figure in the same sort of cloak appeared and called to everybody.

"Once again," said Gaz's recognisably posh voice, "we gather here. Come in now, come in. There have been developments. I hope you're ready for a night of pleasure."

So, it *was* an orgy, then. Vanya was inside that house somewhere. The jealousy she felt physically stung. There were so many thoughts racing through her head. If she could somehow buy a similar black cloak, she could disguise herself and enter the orgy undetected. Like Tom Cruise in *Eyes Wide Shut,* she could see what was happening.

Who was she kidding. She wasn't so far gone that she thought sneaking into the house would win Vanya back. They'd see her amidst all those others, see how fat and poor she was, and they would be disgusted by her presence. So Frankie stood in the dark, watching the figures disappear into the doorway. Her envy had faded, and now all that swirled in her was drunken depression. It was still early enough that she could go somewhere, surely. There was a bar close to here, frequented by desperate lonely men seeking desperate lonely people to fuck. She'd been there many times before, if not for a few years. It had been a spot to turn tricks at when every other place wasn't yielding, a lowest common denominator-type hole. Nobody was happy there, save the students who went purely to piss off the regular clientele. They made her job harder too. The guys would be less willing, might write her off as a student. She had to soothe them, expend more emotional labour just for the chance to suck their dick. She walked back the way she had come and turned off towards the seafront.

The bar was under the arches near the beach. It was open as usual, but the bouncer was new. He didn't recognise her, and he spent far too much time looking at her passport and comparing the passport photograph with her face. *Yeah, I've put on weight since then, so fucking what … Yeah, I'm visibly fucked, so what, everybody who comes here is.* Eventually he shrugged, as if there hadn't been any problem at all. Inside, the bar smelled like piss. *I'm home*, she thought. There were so many men, so many easy gets. *Make me feel like a natural woman. Just for one night, make me feel like that.* It wasn't too much to ask, surely. It was only a quick, kind word or two. A touch, and a kiss on the neck.

4

FERTILITY GODDESS

She could, if she wanted to, write a psychogeographical study of all the bathrooms in all the bars she had sucked dicks in over her years. They were, invariably, men's rooms. They were, invariably, filthy. The only time she herself had received pleasure in a toilet was that first night with Vanya, although perhaps that was a little reductive. There was pleasure in sucking a dick, pleasure in a simple job well done. Like going to a restaurant, ordering the most normie item on a menu, and then finding out it tastes great: the blowjob is just like that. You can half-ass it and receive little to no pushback. You can really put the effort in too. And on this night, she put the effort in, especially in this bathroom, with this man. There was no real reason to put this much care into her craft in this instance, but she did it anyway. His dick was in her mouth. His balls smelled like malt. She felt one of his pubes tickling the back of her throat. And she looked up at him, looking up at him looking down at her, their eyes connecting over his old-man paunch. It wasn't quite what she needed but it was something, so she kept sucking. She might as well. What else was there to do?

~

When she'd first arrived at the bar, there had been lots of guys there, mostly older, busted guys. But only one had looked at her twice. No, he wasn't the best-looking guy in the world, true, but he was the only one who had paid her any attention. What the fuck was that about?

Guys, especially guys like the ones in this bar, would fuck anything they could. Not that long ago she was pulling the Stallion, and now she was sucking *this* guy's dick. He looked like a fucking tortoise. He was easy to get though. She'd just sat there and listened to him talk about his job. He rolled her a fag, he stared at her chest.

"But the interesting thing," he said, "is the way we deal with growth ..."

Frankie smiled a winning, girly smile. *Tell me all about how much you earn again, Daddy, tell me about how rich you are.*

She wasn't well. She was unwell. After they had both smoked a fag, she sat at a table with the man, in a corner, away from the dancefloor. He had put his hand on her thigh, and she'd let him keep it there. Every few minutes his fingers crept a little further up her leg towards her cunt. She hadn't told him she was trans, though given this was a bar mostly for older gay men, she imagined he'd guessed. Still, there was a chance he might be gutted when he found out she didn't have a cock. He was still talking at her, and she didn't think he really cared that she wasn't listening. He'd given her some kind of pill just now, something that tasted bitter. It made his eyes shine brighter; she kissed him suddenly, and he tasted like After Eights.

"What are you?" he asked. His voice floated through the ether to her.

She returned to her old lie. "I'm Jewish."

"I like Jews," he said. "I like money."

~

His cum was bitter. She swallowed it anyway. Then, after he'd gotten his breath back, leaning aginst the cubicle wall, he pissed on her face. It got in her hair and dripped down onto her dress. He didn't tell her he was going to do that, all he said was that she was a good little urinal. And she *was* a good little urinal, she was. She was eager to please and to drink, lick, swallow up every last drop.

She knelt in a puddle of toilet floor water. In it, her reflection looked back at her. Of all the toilets she'd fucked in, of all the puddles she'd seen, this was on the higher end, really. It felt good, then, when he held her hair.

Not looking at him, she spoke, very quietly. "Do you think I'm a bad person?"

"Well ... you seem like a very nice young lady," he said. He must have been wondering what he had gotten himself into.

"*Seem like*," she said. "You don't know me at all. I'm fucking horrible. I drove away my friends, I alienated my partner by pushing them too hard, I lost my job for being a cunt ... I don't have any old friends, you know? Everybody has *old friends*. From school or from their hometown. From uni, even. I don't have any. Everybody I've ever been close to has fucked off ... I've *made* them all fuck off. Can you imagine that?"

He was silent, obviously.

"I scared off the person I was in love with because I wanted them to get me pregnant. How stupid is that? They didn't even have a dick! They didn't have any way of doing it!"

"What?" He looked down at her from on high, like an angel. Bathed in brightness. Perhaps that was just the bulb on the men's loo ceiling, perhaps it was a halo.

"Oh..." She smiled up at him and wiped the tears from her eyes. "I was just getting emotional. Sorry. That wasn't very professional of me."

"But what you said about ... getting you pregnant. What was that?"

He put his fingers underneath her chin and tipped her head back so she could look him in the eyes, through the impossible distance.

"I ... I wanted them to get me pregnant. It's a thing with me ... Do ... Is that something you'd like to do?" It was a stupid question, and there was only one answer.

"It'll be my pleasure," he said.

He tightened his fist around her throat and pushed her into the side of the toilet stall. Her head hit the hard plastic. She was so shocked she didn't even scream. He stood up from the toilet so he could haul her back up. His arms were much stronger than she would have expected: that's what she was thinking about, absurdly, in the moment before he slammed the side of her head into the rim of the toilet. Now she screamed, tried to struggle, but too late. One more hit of her forehead against the ceramic and she was out.

A bit of blood dripped down into the water in the bowl. He left her there, leaning like a dreamer with her head resting on the seat, while he called somebody on his phone. She couldn't move. She heard him speak to someone urgently, telling whoever it was to come and get them.

"I found one," he said. She heard those words, said with childlike joy, and then she passed out completely, bleeding and dribbling away, tongue lolling out of her mouth and resting on the toilet seat. *Lick it up bitch, lick it up.*

5

PISS GHOST

I pissed in a haunted public bathroom the other day, the last public bathroom in Britain, and it was haunted. A girl crying beneath the urinals.

I took my dick out to piss and then suddenly she was there, crouched on the wet floor, and her eyes were yellow and reflected the yellow light and she was looking right up at me, and the yellow was dripping down her cheeks. I felt so sorry for her but there was nothing I could do. I had already started pissing. I couldn't stop, that's not how it works. I couldn't stop so I just had to keep pissing into the urinal while she crouched there, looking up at me. Crying. Yellow.

Once my bladder was empty, I tucked my cock back under my dress and I said honey, are you okay? Is there anything I can do? This isn't the place for a girl like you. Let me wash my hands and I'll take you away from here. This is the men's bathroom. I went and washed my hands and when I came back, she was gone. She was still there, in the walls, in the reflection in the urine puddles, but I could no longer see her.

The day after, I saw it on the news: they demolished it, the last public bathroom in the country. A small crowd turned up to watch its destruction. They cheered when the bricks shattered, and someone let off a party popper. In the brick dust the girl's ghost still crouched before she faded away completely, and I knew I had failed her. The Prime Minister gave a speech stating that s/he was proud to have finally demolished the last public bathroom in the country. No more would Britain by plagued by the monstrous terror presented by free public bathrooms – from now on everyone could rejoice in having to enter the nearest café or restaurant if they wanted to shit, and they could rejoice in having to pay for an overpriced drink or overpriced food just for the right to shit, and this would kickstart the failing economy finally, no more would we be plagued by the terror of public bathrooms, no more would we cower in fear at what they represented: the failure of free public utilities, underfunded, dirty, dangerous, unhygienic, George Michael, men in the women's room and women in the men's, drug deals, not having to pay out money when you're in town and you need to relieve yourself, not having the right to public safety and privacy.

In the final days of the empire, people started cottaging again, and this was the only way to stop it. Dismantling them piece by piece. Cobweb by cobweb. Halogen bulb by halogen bulb.

The people we got to clean them, who knows what happened to them – they were complicit in the whole sordid affair. Perhaps they should be taken somewhere quiet away from everything and *dealt with or perhaps we should just have made them watch as we pulled it all apart. Brick by brick, moment by moment.*

I failed you.

I wished I had taken your hand and exorcised you.

No girl should have to live in a room built for men.

I'm sorry for what happened. I'm sorry I didn't do enough when there was still time, I left it too late and then there was nothing, there was a moment when I faced the choice to either bear the discomfort of trying to stop peeing and help you, or to go on pissing, and I chose the second of those two things and it was the wrong choice and I hope you can forgive me.

And I hope on the site of the last public bathroom they build a grave or a monument but I don't think they will. I think they'll build a Pret and call it a win.

All the things you saw. All the orgasms. All the junkies shooting up because they never opened that safe injection site that they said they would.

The first kisses, the deaths. The slow dancing together beneath the flickering light.

Was this country ever Great? No, but the public toilets were Great, I say, reaching out to you as you fade. The public toilets were Great. I miss them very much. These days if you have to piss you have to hold it in, or piss in a bush somewhere and risk being arrested and done for perversion.

I miss you. You were the last good thing about this shithole, the only good thing it had going – it wasn't Great but you were. Sometimes, very occasionally, against all odds, something Great is produced.

BRAINWYRMS

There are people in the world right now who, through the internet, spread opposition to germ theory – they make videos on YouTube where they sit down and eat rotten meat, and claim it is good for them, claim they enjoy it. There are people who believe they are being watched and that every person around them is secretly employed by some mysterious agency. They don't know why they are being followed. There are secret signals relayed to them in the buzzing of the electricity in their walls, there are secrets you can find if you dig your uncut nails deep enough into your palm: it is possible to see the workings of the world. Perhaps that's why they are stalking you. They're trying to make you die, so you have to not die, right? That's what they'd want. There are men who construct their lives entirely around their whisky collections and women who film their happy domestic lives in their uncanny houses that don't look at all real. Girls convert to Catholicism because of misplaced capitalism-induced malaise and get convinced of the threat of the troons grooming their kids, so they run right into the arms of some monstrous colonial paedophilic revenant, the sort of thing that seems like it should have died one hundred times over and yet lives. We're all running scared – I know I am. My world has shrunk to the size of my own bedroom. The sky used to be a different colour. I could swear it, St Paul's Cathedral used to fill with me awe but now I can barely focus my eyes on it, I'm too distracted by the noise. I wish I found it easier to find beauty and grace, and of course beauty and grace are still there. But everything is fragmented. The people aren't even likeable anymore. I don't find them beautiful. There's no great coming together, no beautiful destruction of borders. There's just a girl being suspended from hooks lodged into her flesh. A bag pulled down over her head so they don't have to look at her. It's just a sex thing. If you look at some weird shit you found, people acting in a way you don't understand, just tell yourself it's a sex thing. Everything's a sex thing, even the things that don't look like sex things. TERFs all get together and wear dinosaur costumes and do shit karaoke and cry in private events rooms. That's a sex thing. They don't know it but it's a sex thing. Guardian *dinner parties are sex things, cabinet meetings are about sex, they're all wearing day collars, they're all wearing lingerie. This doesn't make them degenerate, this makes them just like you. The thing that makes it evil is that they think they're different, they think it isn't a sex thing, they think it's about control. It is, but it's a sex thing. Everything. Those couples that have YouTube prank wars. Those books about plucky elderly people solving crime.* Countdown. *Foxhunting. The rich have always fucked low-class scum like you. This is a sex thing. This book. This act of writing it. Obviously. I'm not exempt but I'm not a hypocrite. It's fine to do a sex thing, but it's best to know it's a sex thing, it's best not to try and make it more than it is. You haven't found a better way of living, you just want to fuck. You haven't seen the future you're just horny and lonely and scared and that's okay, I promise. Everything's going to be fine from here on out, because we're all in this together, and we're all ready to open our hearts and accept that it's falling to pieces. We're all going to die in pain, or worse. We might not die at all. We might live through it. Hold my hand and come with me into the dark.*

6

THE CHAMBER OF SECRETS

"Ah, she's had one too many. I'm just putting her in a taxi."

"Yeah mate. Sure."

Did they not see the blood on her face, in her hair? Did they not care? He held her against him to cover the worst of it, but that could only go so far.

"Now," he said, under his breath, "you're going to get in the car waiting for us. I'm going to put a hood over your head and tie you up. I'm not going to kill you or rape you, I just need you to come with me. If you scream or try to get away, though ... Well, then it'll be a problem."

Into his shoulder, she slurred a sound that she hoped he knew meant she agreed to his terms.

Consciousness was a fickle thing; it came and went as it pleased. She felt the sea breeze outside the bar, and heard the bouncer say goodbye to the man. But after that, she wasn't aware of anything until she was already in the car. The man was on the backseat next to her. He held a fistful of some black fabric in his hand. Another man, sat in the seat behind her, reached around to prop her up. She didn't struggle as they pulled the fabric down over her head. Once it was on, the realisation hit her, and she felt almost as stupid as she felt for getting into this fucking mess: it was a leg of her tights. They'd put her tights over her head, obscuring her face like a bank robber in an old thriller. The smell of her own body odour hit her. This is what she got for not fucking showering for days, this was *penance*. It was so hard to breathe through the tights and talking was nearly impossible. That was the idea, of course, at least in this case. Why the fuck a bank robber would want to wear something this restrictive was anybody's guess, and her concussed mind mused on that while she slipped out of reality again.

The car journey seemed short, although she wasn't awake for all of it. They tied her hands behind her back and put a rope around her neck by which they could lead her. Both men wore black cloaks, and they pulled their hoods up before they exited the car. The first man, the one who had pissed in her mouth, was the one who held the leash. He yanked her out of the car. She sprawled on all fours on the pavement. *Want me to bark when you lead me along like a dog? I'll bark for you Daddy ... I'll do anything for you.* The other man pulled her up, and together the three of them crossed over towards their destination.

The house looked different through the filter of her own worn tights, but it was that same house, of course. She remembered when she approached it before, consensually. How it had looked down at her. And now, again, she felt so small. She might as well be a dog, a tiny yapping thing skittering around their ankles, vulnerable to a wayward boot. The door opened wide for them.

"Tell that little hipster upstart we've got his willing bitch," said the other man, the one she didn't know. She couldn't see who he was talking to.

"You're unlucky," said the one who walked her. "He's been looking for someone just like you, see. Needs someone who can get pregnant and, more importantly, who wants to be."

If she'd been able to open her mouth properly to tell him that she *couldn't* get pregnant, no matter how hard she tried, she wouldn't have bothered. At this point they were probably going to kill her either way. But they'd definitely kill her if they found out she wasn't any use. That was sound logic, even to a concussed slut like her, shivering and bloodied, her tights ripped from her legs.

The hall of the house was dead. She stumbled her way along, sometimes walking crouched over, sometimes crawling. Through a doorway they dragged her. This room hadn't been open when she was here before, she was sure of that. There was a pool table in the middle of it, and antlers hanging on a wall. At the far end of the room, two figures in cloaks stood guard on either side of another doorway.

"Good specimen," said one, looking at her as she crouched on the floor, panting in shallow breaths through the nylon.

"He'll be happy," said the other. "Looks like a right slut. She'll probably take anything."

They opened the door. Through it was darkness. She could just about see some rough-hewn stone steps dropping downwards, spiralling around a bend and out of sight. There was a faint smell of sulphur, which grew as their little party of travellers approached the stairs. By the time they were through the door, and she was scrambling down the cold bricks of those steps, the smell was strong enough to make her gag: rotten eggs, farts, bile. There was no respite from it, not even brief pockets of fresh air. Single lightbulbs hung from the ceiling, but only occasionally: much of the time they were pulling her down into the semi-darkness. Often, she fell, scraping the skin from her arms and legs. At a certain point the two men became very frustrated with her inability to walk properly. It hurt so much, and with each fall it hurt more and became more difficult to even think about taking a step. After she crumpled onto the ground and would not move, they picked her up between them and carried her roughly the rest of the way.

Her head was turned towards the ceiling. She watched as bulbs passed by, sometimes with insects banging themselves against the hot glass. The stairs went on. Round and round, down and down. Into the depths of the earth. That sulphur smell: that was the smell of hell, she thought. Hell wasn't something she believed in, but if anybody deserved to be dragged there it was her, at least by her own judgement. For being such a fucking *creep*, for being so corrosive and caustic that everybody left her. This was her punishment. To be carried down into the dark.

Then, quite suddenly, the ceiling changed. Frankie tilted her head down just enough to see that they were in a low room, made of the same bare stone as the stairway. It was about the same size as a church crypt, and much like a church crypt it was laid out with pillars to support the weight of the world that lay atop it.

That really was how it felt. This was the *underneath*, she thought. The foundation that lay at the roots of the whole world. The chamber of secrets on which the pile of shit and stone was constructed. And down here they gathered to enjoy their spoils, to writhe around in the dirt. The men threw her brutally onto the bare, dusty floor.

Fuck. Frankie, don't let them see how much it hurts. Don't ...

At her presence, the crowd turned. A hundred hungry eyes peering down at her from decrepit faces. A voice spoke. Posh. Generations of hate stored in every syllable. "And what is this you have bought for us?"

Her kidnapper, the one she had been with in the toilet, replied. "A willing female was requested. Here is one."

Gaz stepped from out of the shadows.

"Oh ..." He bent down over her, stroked her face. He cooed, as one might over a newborn.

"Oh, she's perfect," he said. He was crouched right next to her head. His naked cock was right in her eyeline.

They were all naked. Everybody down here. Far too many people for her to count. Naked and free.

When Gaz was done inspecting her, he stood back up, lithe and catlike. Like a cat he turned to a crowd that was nestled between the columns, awaiting his words.

"Friends ... this may well be the night. When my father introduced me to this world, I was overjoyed to be welcomed into this club. It was eye-opening, that was for sure. But I always felt there was more to do, a way to use these gifts we are privilege to. I know some of you think I'm an idiot, with my endless theories and plans. But I suppose we'll find out if I am now, won't we?"

"You've done well, son," said one of the oldest men in the group. He shuffled out into a clearing in the middle of the chamber, a clearing surrounded by columns and watching bodies. He was so elderly that the short journey to his son's side took an eternity. If Frankie had been in any state to laugh, she would have. She would have laughed as the old man scuffed his bare feet across the dusty ground. His body was so wrinkled that the liver-spotted skin of his belly was indistinguishable from the skin on his balls. Gaz got tired of waiting for him and just met him halfway so they could embrace. He gripped his father tightly.

"I wouldn't have done it without you, Daddy."

"I'm very proud of you," said the old man, hugging Gaz back in return. The effort was rough for him, obviously. He hugged Gaz so hard that his whole body shook, like a dog shitting. When they were joined like that, their cocks, both semi-flaccid, touched, and twitched.

The doorway back to the stairs was too far for Frankie to get to without somebody seeing. If her arms weren't fucking tied, maybe she could have pushed some reaching hands away from her, but as it was, there was no chance. It would have been hard enough to pull herself to her feet.

From the other direction, she heard a little gasp. She turned back to see Gaz's father kneeling on the ground. His son's cock was in his mouth.

What the fuck.

"We usually did this the other way around," said Gaz, between little moans of pleasure. "I suppose I've ... I've earned it, right? Well, everyone. Let's get to work. You all know what you have to do."

Fuck. When Frankie was a little girl, her stepfather had come home one night, drunk as he'd ever been. He'd come into her room, swaying, nearly falling. His big body had blocked out her nightlight. "Look," he'd said, "You're grown enough now to understand, why do you look so grim all the time? Why do you look so half-dead? You think your life sucks? You suck, you suck, I'll give you something to suck, see, see ...". Born with a dick in her brain, and worse. Born with a dick.

Gaz's Dad sucked his son's dick with a startling enthusiasm. He took it deep into the back of his throat. The old guy still had it, then. He could barely walk, but he still had it where it counted.

The crowd surged forwards with excitement. Suddenly she found herself surrounded by flesh, almost all of it pale, almost all of it wrinkled, although there were some younger people, and some who had undergone surgery to stay as young as they could. From where she lay, she saw them at the most unflattering angle imaginable. She saw dicks small and large, balls drooping so low they must have brushed against their owner's knees. Tits with large, aged nipples, and tits with implants, and even a couple of tits that were round and young.

"Ladies and gentleman," Gaz said. "You all know this world is sick. You don't feel at home anymore. It used to be better, it's all falling apart. Even as recent as twenty-twelve, with the Olympics, things at least felt *coherent*. That was the last time we felt like a real country, a place to take pride in. Whatever your ideology, you can agree on that, correct? That the world is sick. So let us experience the pleasure we deserve and let us *use it* to create a world not sick, a world where we can freely and openly experience this without the disgust of those proles who would never understand. Let us fuck, let us fuck together as one, and be food for the worms."

The crowd pulled him and his father down to the ground. They surged over Frankie too. Her kidnappers must have stripped off, because she saw the face of one of them right near her, and he was kissing some woman who she could have sworn was in the shadow cabinet. As they kissed, *things* reached from his eyes to hers. When their mouths pulled apart, the same things were there, like strings of spit, but moving. There were hands on her, touching her all over. Digging, long fingernails deep enough to draw blood. Naked bodies rolled together on top of her, fucking. The air was thick with moans.

Low moans and high gasps, guttural growls of deep pleasure and little squeals of delight. Frankie lay on her back, facing the ceiling. It was old and riddled with cracks. Cracks in the foundation. Was the world going to collapse in on this place and bury them all alive?

Her tears soaked into the nylon that shrouded her, but her screams were muffled, no matter how loud they were. For all she knew, her cries might have sounded like the sounds of pleasure, might have sounded like the ecstatic response to some *Guardian* journalist shoving her fingers up into Frankie's cunt, as was happening now. Somebody else grabbed her neck and tightened, not enough to choke her, really, but enough to make her head swim.

After what her stepfather did, Frankie had gone to her Mum. "He made me do things," she said, resting on her shoulder "I don't know why." But her mother shrugged her off. "Don't say things like that about your father. He took you in when you had nobody, we took you in when you were all alone." Eventually, running away felt easier than staying, so that was what she did. It had been a hot and muggy night, and halfway across town the sky had split open and rain came down. But it was too late to turn back by then. So, she kept running. She ran all the way here, she supposed. To this dusty floor below a house in Kemptown, beneath a living mass of fucking rich cunts. Maybe her stepfather was somewhere here in this crowd. He wasn't rich back then, but maybe he'd gotten rich, like he always said he would. Maybe he'd won the lottery or invested in something fruitful.

Something wet touched the bare skin of her hand. She couldn't see what it was; her hand was pinned under the full weight of people's bodies pressed together. But the wetness grew, the feeling spreading. Had they cum so soon? That was the best explanation for the wetness, she knew. But she also suspected that wasn't what she could feel, dripping onto her arm.

A face pushed into her view, right above her, looking down into her obscured eyes.

Oh fuck. She knew that face. She knew every fucking inch of it. She knew those blue eyes and that *fucking* smirk. Every kid her age that grew up in this stupid country knew it intimately, from the dustjackets of all those books and then from her profile picture on Twitter. But it was one thing seeing an image and quite another having that same face looming over her. She stopped screaming and just stared up in horror. *Oh, if only you knew how much I hate you, if only you knew what I tweeted at you, if only you knew.*

Her hands grasped at Frankie's body. Her fingernails drew blood.

Jennifer fucking Caldwell. The Saint. The warrior-priestess. The cancelled Queen. On all fours on top of her. Somebody ate her cunt from behind, and they in turn were getting pleasure from others.

Jennifer's smirk became a smile. Then the smile grew wider than was natural, and her lips parted, revealing a mouth full of writhing white worms. The worms were in her eyes too. They were hanging from her nostrils. She vomited a tidal wave of them down over Frankie's face. The liquid tasted like that drink Gaz had given her – it was sweet in the same way, and thick. The worms slipped all over her face, trying to push through the fabric and into her mouth.

She looked to her left and saw others gushing worms out of their mouths too. Some of them dripped fat ones from their eyes. One man squeezed them out of his urethra and onto two women crouching below him. The women waited, open mouthed and eager eyed. On her right she saw the same scenes. People exchanging the things inside of them. They left thick, living threads between each other, connecting everybody without prejudice.

Jennifer was laughing.

"Oh, it feels so good!" she said. Whatever control she might have had over her excretion of the worms was now gone. They flowed out of her eyes, dripping down her sagging cheeks. "It feels so good, I could cry."

Frankie didn't want to look. She risked a glance, just one, and that was enough. She screwed her eyes shut and screamed. That wasn't a face, not now. No eyes. No cheeks. No lips. None of the discrete parts that the human brain recognised as a face. Where there had once been a recognisably human visage, however hateful, there was now only a kaleidoscopic burst of worms. If they were worms ... She wasn't sure at this point. She wasn't sure of anything. Perhaps they were tongues without jaws, or the severed cocks of an entire forgotten pantheon. Caldwell's head looked like a flower opening in the midday sunlight, but the petals were wet, they were horribly alive, and they were all over her, pushing into her, filling her with ideas she didn't want, filling her up until she was fit to burst. And at the very heart of it all was a light, burning out from the centre of where the author's face should have been. A blinding, beautiful white light, out of which the worms tumbled into this ragged world.

The light ... Where before this chamber had been dark, now there was light. A great, blinding light shining through the doorway. It hurt to look at it, but it hurt to look at anything, so she kept staring into its whiteness, even as she felt someone pulling her legs apart, and something wet on her thighs, and then ...

~

When she ran away from home, the man she ended up with dressed her like a doll and called her perfect. It was then that she knew she was a girl. She'd suspected it before, of course, but it was when he fucked her like a doll that she knew for sure. "Oh you poor China girl", he said when he'd cum in her. "Have I cracked your face?" She assured him it was fine, she wasn't that fragile, she'd had beatings far rougher than that. "I wish you had a cunt," he said. "You'd be so pretty if you had a cunt." Yes, she agreed. She agreed with that. His bed smelled like cinnamon, and the ceilings in his flat were too high. The day he killed himself, she'd tried to talk to him, and he didn't even remember her name. He told her she should stay away from him because he was violent. He knew he was, he knew that someday soon he'd lose control and hurt a kid, a very young one. She just had to get out of there before it was too late. *Please don't, I don't have anywhere else to go, please I'm adrift don't you see you're the only person I have I can't get back out on the streets I wanted to feel your cum in my cunt one day I wanted to feel it dripping out of me I want your babies I'd have your babies you didn't hurt me I wanted it its ok* but he locked the door, locked her out of the room. No matter how hard she pummelled her fists against the wood it didn't change anything. By the time the ambulance got there he was spasming with a needle in his arm, foaming from the mouth. Now, thinking back, she saw worms in the foam that came out. Worms dripping down onto his bedsheets. Worms laced in his fancy curtains, in the clothes in his closet. That was a lie though. There had been no worms then, there was just the room he'd once been in and where now he wasn't.

~

Hands tore the tights away from Frankie's face. Jennifer leaned back. She sat astride Frankie, and her bare cunt opened up, a gaping maw from which spurted a fountain of worms.

"Frankie?" There. A voice. From somewhere within the forest of limbs.

"Vanya?"

Jennifer growled. Then Vanya was there, pushing Jennifer away, putting their skinny arms around her.

"Frankie, oh my God, it's you, I'm so ... I'm so sorry ... I didn't know ..."

There was screaming. People, still joined together, started to realise something was wrong. Gaz tried to push through them, but his progress was hindered by how many of them were still happily fucking, oblivious to the problems.

"Fucking fat tranny," he snarled. "No, no this isn't right, you can't get pregnant, no ..."

Vanya pulled with all their strength. "I need you to get up. I need you to stand, I need you to run for the door. Can you do that?"

"Yes," she said. "Please, please ..."

Vanya hauled Frankie to her feet. Jennifer Caldwell clawed at her ass, but her fingers slipped right off Frankie's slick skin. Vanya and Frankie stumbled on, Frankie's hands still bound behind her. The light was close. The only way out, even if it was painful, even if it was boiling hot. They ran into it, as the crowd howled with displeasure. That howling was the last thing they heard before the brightness took over and became everything. The entire world, white and empty. And then there was the hard, dark ground beneath them. The thick sea lapping at the shore. The strange cries of unseen things. A sky the colour of a cadaver's skin.

7

COCKLESS GODS

They lay together for a while on the ground, quite still. When Frankie felt able to, she sat up. There was nothing out to sea, nothing inland. Nothing but the occasional worm slithering to who knows where.

Vanya's eyes were closed. They looked peaceful, at least to her. Peaceful and still. So beautiful. She bent down to Vanya and kissed their lips. Their eyes shot open, and they shoved her away.

"Get the fuck off me! What's wrong with you, Frankie. I saved your fucking life, and you just do that?"

Frankie shrunk down like a snail hiding in its shell. "You ... I'm sorry, you just looked really pretty. I'm sorry, I didn't mean to ... I didn't mean to hurt you I'm sorry I'm sorry."

She looked so pathetic. So scared. So alone. "Where are we?" She whimpered.

"I don't know."

"It's ... It hurts to look around."

"The worms aren't from earth. This is the country they come from. I don't know where it is. Gaz showed it to me once. I glimpsed it in the light."

"Don't be stupid," she said. "We're just ... I don't know. Somewhere up the coast. Someone must have knocked us out or made us hallucinate with drugs or something."

Vanya looked at her like she was *nothing*. There was no care or nostalgia in that look. The look said *shut the fuck up*. Frankie did.

"If we walk long enough, we might find a way back," they said. "I can't promise anything. I'm not from here. We might just end up walking forever and dying of starvation. Something might eat us. But I won't have you just staying here feeling sorry for yourself. Come on."

Vanya picked a direction along the coastline and started to walk, not looking behind them yet being careful to listen for Frankie's footsteps. Yes, she was there. She was following.

Frankie kept asking questions. Vanya answered them when they felt like answering, which was rarely. They told her about how they'd met Gaz, about their respective interests. They told her what he'd said after the breakup: his father and all their rich friends gave themselves these strange brain parasites, and he believed he had been experimenting with them to see if they could be *used* for something. But that was all Vanya knew, really. Gaz had wanted someone to impregnate, but Vanya didn't know why. It didn't matter. Frankie couldn't get pregnant, so whatever he'd been planning wouldn't have worked.

They walked in silence. They didn't know where they were going. This place was deserted apart from the worms, and if the worms were intelligent, they didn't show it.

Then, after a while, Frankie's stomach started to swell.

~

"It's a fucking miracle," Frankie said, smiling.

So, it would come true, then. This is what he'd said would happen, but you hadn't believed him. You'd thought he was deluded, horny, and stupid, thinking that his dick made him a genius. But now here you were.

"Vanya," she said. "I was shit to you. I was really shit."

"Hush, it's okay. You don't need to speak."

"I ... I saw about your Mum. I realised what had happened. I was the girl she nearly killed in the bombing. I was confused and traumatised, I'm sorry."

"Frankie, shh. I barely knew her, and I hated her. I was sad about my family, but I'm fine. I knew about you. Stop wasting your energy. You'll need it for the birth."

Frankie grinned. There were tears on her face. "I never thought I'd feel this."

"Just breathe. I forgive you if that matters. I forgive you." You weren't sure you did, but it felt like the right thing to say.

"Really?"

"Yes. I forgive you. Hold my hand now. It'll be okay."

"God it hurts."

"I know."

Her belly had swollen even larger. The skin was starting to split around her belly button.

"I ... I'm going to be a Mummy," she said. "I always wanted that. I always wanted to be pregnant, I always thought it would feel good. It does feel good. It hurts, but it feels good. It feels so good. I wish you would touch my cunt, but maybe you shouldn't ... I don't know what's happening down there ..." She winced.

You looked. Her cunt was gaping wider and wider. There was white light shining through.

"It'll be alright," you said. "It's coming along fine."

"Is this normal?"

"Yes."

"I'm sorry I hurt you," she said. "I shouldn't have hurt you. I ... It feels so... Oh my God, it feels like heaven. Oh my God," she gasped. "I think I'm going to cum."

She screamed, and her cunt split open with a burst of bright red blood. It tore, from her arsehole all the way up to her abdomen. Both her legs flopped down on either side of her, and her body went stiff and still. There were still breaths in her mouth, but they were fading.

From the great tear in her body, it uncoiled. It was huge, so huge that you didn't know how it had grown inside of her. So, this was it. The thing Gaz said would rain down terror upon the world. The great oppressor, an enemy that humanity could be united in its stand against. He'd told you to mother it, to nurse it, to bring it home when it was grown, when it was filled with all the hate against the world that it could carry. Could you do that? Was it worth it? Would a war tearing the planet apart fix everything? You weren't a political theorist, how were you to know? Those questions were beyond you. You just did what you were told.

The great white wyrm spiralled up into the sky, but its eyes were cast down towards you. Oh, you opened your arms to it. Oh, my child, my lovely one. I know you're scared. I'm scared too. Come here now. Come here. This pain and fear you feel, let me tell you why you feel it: there's a country called Britain, far away from here. The people there, they hurt you. They did this to you. One day you'll go back there. One day you'll make them pay. When you arrive, they'll be killing each other. One day you'll get your revenge. But for now, curl around me and let me sing you a song to sleep. You'll need the rest. Let me sing you a song. Let's see if I can remember.

"Out – out are the lights – out all!
  And, over each quivering form,
The curtain, a funeral pall,
  Comes down with the rush of a storm,
While the angels, all pallid and wan,
  Uprising, unveiling, affirm
That the play is the tragedy, 'Man,'
And its hero, the Conqueror Worm."
That's you, my darling one. My conqueror worm.

ABOUT THE AUTHOR

ALISON RUMFITT is a writer, semiprofessional trans woman, and the author of *Tell Me I'm Worthless.* Her debut pamphlet of poetry, *The T(y)ranny,* was a critical deconstruction of Margaret Atwood's work through the lens of a trans woman navigating her own misogynistic dystopia. Her work has appeared in countless publications, such as *Sporazine, Data-bleed, Bloody Women, Burning House Press, Soft Cartel, Glass: A Journal of Poetry,* and more. Her poetry was nominated for the Rhysling Award in 2018. You can find her on Twitter @hangsawoman and on Instagram @alison.zone. She loves her friends.